"*Angelwalk* packs a whallop! I read it fascinated—charmed by its style, shaken by its message, and in the end inspired. A brave and beautiful book I'll be recommending the rest of my life."

–Marjorie Holmes

"More than a novel, *Angelwalk* is an experience. We relive the past and witness the future. Elwood's work is highly imaginative. He skillfully sharpens our awareness of the hideousness of sin, and forces us to be realistic about its consequences. *Angelwalk* is full of issues that need to be attacked. The author compels us to face these in this intelligent and provocative work. Highly recommended."

–Ruth Narramore

"*Angelwalk* is not only a really good book, well done throughout, but it is also a much needed one. Too often people tend to proclaim their beliefs in a quite shallow, often flippant manner; it is safe and easy for them to do so. Very powerful and gripping, *Angelwalk* forces us to come to terms with the troubling realities of our times, and to attest to our faith in a crucible of uncompromising honesty."

–George Gallup, Jr.

"An unquestionably excellent work, with powerful insights into modern thinking."

–*The Baptist Sentinel*

"*Angelwalk* is a sustained work of the imagination. Roger Elwood is to be highly commended."

–Myrna Grant, Wheaton College Graduate School

"Every so often a book comes along that perfectly captures the spirit of the age, yet remains relevant for generations to come. *Pilgrim's Progress* and *The Screwtape Letters* are two such books. To put *Angelwalk* in that exalted company may seem presumptuous, but it is not. Roger Elwood has done what every good novelist hopes to do—he has written a book that is both accessible and enduring."

–Robert Silvers, *The Saturday Evening Post*

"*Angelwalk* is in the vein of John Bunyan's *Pilgrim's Progress* and C. S. Lewis's *Screwtape Letters*. Roger Elwood has the same kind of insight to truth as Bunyan and Lewis and very few others."

–W. S. McBirnie, bestselling author of
Search for the Twelve Apostles

"Roger Elwood comes as close to duplicating Lewis's achievement as any recent writer has."

–Harold Lindsell

"What a terrific book! I kept weeping and would have to stop and pray and ponder parts of the book as I went along. I trust that the Lord is going to use it to wake people up to eternity."

–Debra Evans, author

"Roger Elwood is an artist whose brush is words. This linguistic painting is filled with range, scope, deep spiritual meaning and inspiring promise. It was my pleasure and spiritual enrichment to have participated in a seminar with C. S. Lewis at Oxford. His *Screwtape Letters* was first introduced there and has since of course become a legendary fantasy. *Angelwalk* has that same feel. It just may be that another C. S. Lewis is among us."

–Jess Moody, author and pastor
First Baptist Church, Van Nuys, California

"A striking work! Does an excellent job of presenting sin in its true colors without the sugarcoated treacherous cover Satan gives it to lure people from God. Reminiscent of *Screwtape Letters* and *Pilgrim's Progress,* this modern fable takes a graphic look at the pain and destruction people have brought on themselves and others. *Angelwalk* is a hard book to put down. It's frightening in its picture of the dark forces, yet encouraging in its affirmation of God as the Supreme Ruler."

–*The Bookstore Journal*

"*Angelwalk* is one of the most controversial Christian books of this century. Read it and you'll never be the same again. Roger Elwood has brilliantly woven an impassioned, heartrending story. It would be all too overpowering if it were not for the triumph of our Lord's love shining through the darkness, bringing answers to the world's seemingly hopeless situation—answers wrapped in God's infinite mercy and love, through His Son, Jesus Christ. The reader will become part of *Angelwalk,* as each page leads like a blazing, beckoning beacon on a journey out of darkness into the brilliant light of that day when the lion will lie down with the lamb."

–Joan Winmill Brown, author and actress

"Wonderful—I have never before read anything quite like *Angelwalk.* I think it may be the most unique Christian book published in my lifetime. And it affected me more than just about any other. I was shaken as well as uplifted while reading it. The most impressive aspect of all is how it gives such incredible glory to our Lord throughout, pointing people to Him in a very compelling way. *Angelwalk* deserves to be one of the abiding classics, and I think that is how it will be judged over the years."

–Paul Schumacher, noted gospel singer

"I loved it. *Angelwalk* gets at some crucial truths in a fresh and revealing way. The result is a terrific book. I do wonder how many of us in our daily walk—and, yes, I include myself—would have the kind of bravery that enabled the author to confront Satan head-on, and be as honest about it as he has been.

–Dr. Richard LeTourneau

"*Angelwalk* is a unique and interesting way of conveying Scriptural truth—beautifully written and deeply meaningful."

–Dr. J. Allen Blair

"I have never before read a book quite like *Angelwalk*. It seems to me a return to the literary quality of the days of Shakespeare, almost as though a writer of that era had been transported to this present day and allowed to comment on the world in which we live. It is perhaps the most imaginative Christian book written in this century, and yet it is not a book beyond the average person. In fact, part of the genius of *Angelwalk* is how it takes everyday happenings and deals with them in a way that is understandable to everyone. *Angelwalk* will be, I am sure, a welcome artistic masterpiece for those concerned with the downward trend in the quality of books today, and also a vivid, startling epic of the times for others who view our present society now as very close to its death throes. It stands where I have stood since 1962, namely, against the pervasive corruption of the values on which our country was originally founded."

–Mike Parkhurst, President
Independent Truckers Association

"*Angelwalk* is a most stimulating work of spiritual truth. It takes the mask off what many people would prefer to hide, and it brings them 'front-and-center' with the fact that a personal decision must be made in choosing Christ or Satan. Roger Elwood has found a way to strip away dangerous ignorance and half-truths in this spiritual warfare and expose compromise for what it is."

—Shirley Maxwell, Founder/President
Perfect Peace Ministries, Inc.

Wonderful . . . extremely powerful. I was deeply, deeply moved, and astonished at the scope. A genuinely affecting and masterful work."

—Efrem Zimbalist, Jr.

ANGELWALK

A modern fable

by

Roger Elwood

God spared not the angels that sinned,
but cast them down to hell,
and delivered them into chains of darkness . . .

—*II PETER 2:4*

CROSSWAY BOOKS • WHEATON, ILLINOIS
A DIVISION OF GOOD NEWS PUBLISHERS

Cover illustration by Ron DiCianni.

First printing, 1988

Fifteenth printing, 1995

Printed in the United States of America

Library of Congress Catalog Card Number 87-70456

ISBN 0-89107-440-6

*For Francis A. Schaeffer
—Met Too Briefly But Remembered
for a Lifetime*

FOREWORD

Crossway Books is to be congratulated on the publication of *Angelwalk,* by Roger Elwood. It is an unusual theme and an unusual treatment of a subject that will fascinate the reader and open new vistas along the line of imaginative fiction.

An angel is faced with the choice of joining Satan in his revolt against the God of all creation or of remaining faithful to the One who made him. He is given an opportunity to visit the earth and see and appreciate in advance what the consequences would be if he chooses to follow Satan. His quest is our quest and his experiences our experiences, but what follows the reader will discover for himself as he reads the book. This should whet the appetite of all of us.

Elwood treads in line with the footprints of perhaps the best known writer of this genre—C. S. Lewis, whose *Screwtape Letters* and Narnia Tales have brought him lasting acclaim. For anyone to come near to the heights that C. S. Lewis reached is hard to believe.

Elwood comes as close to duplicating Lewis's achievement as any recent writer has. His background has fitted him well for the task he undertakes. He has a gift for words, a sensitivity to the current milieu, a solid Biblical commitment, and a strong desire to reverse the tide of paganism which is sweeping through the West. He reflects the thesis C. S. Lewis propounded so ably in what I think to be one of his finest works, *The Abolition of Man.*

The reading public will be the final judge of Elwood's effort. And one can hope that his volume will challenge a younger generation of writers to devote their skills to writing fiction in the service of God.

Harold Lindsell

"If Satan himself goes disguised as an angel of light, there is no need to be surprised when his servants, too, disguise themselves as the servants of righteousness"

—2 Corinthians 11:14, 15, JB

I CANNOT AGE, BUT I DO FEEL
somehow old as I sit here, on a mountaintop
overlooking the plain where the last great battle of Mankind has taken place. The bodies
number into the thousands, and blood collects everywhere—giant, deep pools like a titanic wave over the
ground, submerging it. It is possible to drown in blood
down there . . .

I momentarily turn away, the odor so strong that it
ascends the mountain. I try to close my ears because the
cries of the dying are loud enough to form a crescendo
that also reaches me—but there is no escaping the pan-
orama below, either in its sights or its sounds.

I decide to leave the mountain and go down to the

plain where the old prophecies always had been pointing with devastating clarity.

Some of the dying have had the flesh literally seared from their bones, and they have only seconds left, those that survived at all. They see me, of course—the living do not—but those nearly dead, suspended, in a sense, between two kinds of life indeed see, reach out, beg.

"Please help me, sir," I am asked again and again.

"The pain . . ."

"I know I've been blinded, now, yet I see you anyway. I see—"

Ahead, standing as though on an island uplifted in the midst of a blood-red sea, are several hundred soldiers, but no longer with weapons, their former bodily shells lying at their feet.

I approach them.

"We could not continue," one of them tells me. "All of us asked for God's forgiveness through Jesus the Christ."

"There is no doubt that many of our comrades are doomed," another adds, "because of their allegiance to the Devil. We bid them good-bye . . ."

One by one they ascend. The final soldier turns to me, smiles, says, "We did the right thing."

I nod.

. . . we did the right thing.

Yes, they did—all of them—that one group of hundreds out of countless thousands.

They refused the Antichrist. And he had them slaughtered as a result, threatening to do just that once again to any others who might decide to rebel.

And now—

Not one of them bore the scars of how they died—

no bayonet wounds, no bullet holes. In their resurrection they had been healed, given the bodies that would be theirs throughout eternity.

But the others share not at all the same end. Every few seconds, more are dying. Bodies piled upon bodies, visible where the blood is not quite deep enough to hide them. I look about, and see hands raised against the sky, like stalks of marsh grass in a bloody inlet. For an instant only. Then cut down.

They also see me. They surround me as I go past, trying not to look at them, their eyes haunted where they yet have eyes. Some do not, seared away, only the empty sockets remain. But they see me just the same. And all turn away, knowing *they* will spend eternity like that—in agony, flames searing them but never fully consuming.

The scene oppresses. I cannot stand it any longer. I leave, not sure of where to go. I have time at my disposal. I can do whatever I want with it, yes, even choose to stay where I am—in this time and place—or retreat through the centuries, their contents disgorged at my very feet.

And yet, in a way that is beyond mere loneliness—oh, how wonderful if it were but a question of being merely *lonely*—I have nowhere to go. An irony that presses me down inflicts on me a weariness that is so pervasive it is as though all of history has become a singular weight from which it is well-nigh impossible to extricate myself. And I think, in tremulous recollection, of all that preceded this moment, this literal battlefield on which I find myself.

Lord, I whisper with prayerful intent against the dissipating sounds of the vanquished. *My dear, dear Lord.*

The beginning.

WE ARE SITTING BY A CRYSTAL LAKE. A hint of violets surrounds us with its gentle scent.

"Do you know what I used to feel really guilty about on earth?"

The question is asked by a man who had been a show business agent during his mortal life.

"I would be interested in learning about it," I tell him with full sincerity.

He smiles as he says, "When I worked with clients on Broadway, I met plenty of angels, but they weren't like you at all."

We both enjoy the humor of that and then he adds, "My conscience hit me hard, in those days, for two reasons: One, the type of individual with whom I often had to work. I remember the guy who headed one of the studios—one of the most promiscuous homosexuals in a town where being gay was almost an advantage. One day, he invited me to a party given by a producer. I went, against my better judgment. What I encountered was loathsome—open perverted activity, the consumption of illegal drugs, blasphemous jokes, and much more. Many of the offenders were extremely influential in the entertainment business. They had a stranglehold on what the public *saw* in theatres and on television.

"The second area of difficulty was when I had to pass judgment on people, when I had to decide who was or wasn't worthy. Now I know that all of us are worthwhile in the sight of God, that He is concerned about every creation of His, whether a sparrow in the field or a jet pilot or even an agent. But in those days I earned my living in an environment that paid lip service to values and honor and integrity and self-image but in the end created the conditions for the destruction of each of those.

"So there I was, looking at this actor or that one, and I would have to say that one would make it big in the profession, and another might as well quit early. Again and again I played a kind of god game with those kids.

"Actually most took it well, better than I would have, while others did not—but then something happened that changed the whole rat race for me."

"What was that?" I ask.

"I met this exceptionally handsome young actor—tall, attractive and, yes, extremely talented. He was a real contender for the starring role in a potent new TV series. Then someone else came by, and he seemed just right also. I had to choose between them."

"So what was the difference between that incident and any of the others?"

"I had to turn down the first young man. He took it hard, so hard in fact that he shot himself to death less than a week later. He left a suicide note that read, 'I have no worth as a human being. I have nothing. I am nothing. I return to nothing.'

"I was never the same after that. About a month later I accepted Christ as Savior and Lord because I realized that *I* felt very, very worthless at that point, that the only redemption for me was that which the Lord purchased with His shed blood at Calvary."

He pauses, looking at the lake, its surface sparkling like the diamonds described by poets.

"I will never again have to judge another human being. And I myself have been judged and found acceptable in the sight of Almighty God."

He stands, smiling.

"I've just arrived, and would like to experience more of what I could only dream about back on Earth. Would you excuse me, Darien? That is your name, isn't it?"

"Yes," I say simply.

He walks off, cherubs dancing at his feet.

I wish . . .

The words are unspoken, thought only.

I turn and go in another direction. Soon I am talking to people born mentally retarded who now have minds like Augustine or Luther. And the parents who deeply loved them, who stayed with them, who shared the anguish because of their steadfast faith that "all things work together for good"—these parents have been repaid a thousand times, for what carnal life denied them is fully realized in Heaven; children with whole minds and bodies, children who can converse properly and walk without assistance.

I wish I could accept . . .

"If Heaven offered only that," one mother tells me, "it would be worth everything."

Those born without limbs or those who lost arms or legs or hands through accidents are now restored. They have been "repaired." One woman who had never had any limbs at all and who remained a human oddity all her life can now walk about, jumping, running, and shaking hands with everyone, her face aglow.

Those once blind can see and stroll through the parks and gardens, looking with astonishment; those once deaf just sit and listen; those born mute gather in little groups and chatter away.

I wish I could accept all this without . . .

I meet a man known informally as "the Intellectual." He greets me with abundant enthusiasm.

"There was a time when I would have labelled all this as abject nonsense," he admits. "Strolling through Heaven! Saying hello to an angel! There was a time when I would have—"

He interrupts himself, saying, "I looked at life as a uniformity of natural causes in a closed system. How could God, if He existed, which, of course, wasn't the case . . . how could God suddenly reach down into that system anytime He desired, and bring about the Incarnation, the parting of the Red Sea, the healing of lepers? No! I said to myself and to others. A thousand times no! Any thought of the supernatural was sheer idiocy and I would have no part of it.

"I lived in a kind of cocoon, refusing to acknowledge that anything at all existed outside it. What I couldn't see, feel, hold, or reason out didn't exist as far as I was concerned.

"And God as a concept simply failed to compute, as I said back on Earth. He threw my entire equation out, and since that was the case, I ended up throwing Him out because that equation and the scientific concepts from which it originated were my life's foundation. That was what I worshipped, not pie-in-the-sky puffery."

"What changed you?" I ask.

"It was the strangest moment, frankly. I owned a private plane. I was out in it one day, alone. Something malfunctioned in the motor. I saw smoke. The plane nosedived. There was no possibility, considering the elevation and how fast it was falling, that I would survive.

"I prayed then. I know, in looking back, how extraordinary that was. Me, the atheist—I prayed! I had heard all about so-called foxhole Christians and I had scorned their weakness, their instability, yes, their hypocrisy. And yet I was doing the same thing.

"Well, I survived, sustaining remarkably few injuries, certainly nothing serious. As I climbed out of the wreckage of that plane, my first thought was about how little pain I felt! I had some cuts, some bruises, but nothing else.

"I was, of course, glad to be alive. But the fact that I *was* alive stunned me. I examined all my safe, scientific theories, computed in my mind the *logical* possibility that I would *be* alive, and yet nothing supported the reality I was experiencing at that moment which was, simply, my survival.

"I remembered that quick, strangely instinctive prayer. Nothing else could have explained what had happened. God had stepped into my closed world, penetrated my humanistic cocoon—and given me a life that, according to the proper computerized readout, should have been wiped out.

"But you know, that wasn't all. I learned something else. I learned the meaning of His forgiveness, the validity of it, the depth of it. I had spent much of my adult life trying to convince others that He was simply a myth and that Karl Marx had had it right when he called religion an opiate for the masses. I *destroyed* the faith of thousands, you know. And yet God chose to forgive me. I was driven to tears as I understood the significance of that. I closed myself off from everyone for weeks. When I emerged from that self-imposed solitude, I became like Saul of Tarsus. The new me was St. Paul, dedicated to the Kingdom, not bent on causing it to crumble."

We talk a bit more, and then he goes off. Isaac Newton is waiting for him . . .

I wish I could accept all this without the questions, one after the other.

Now I am standing beside a golden sea. The waters are pure, clear; birds swoop overhead. No longer is it necessary for them to kill in order to survive. One of them lands next to me, and walks up to me. I run my hand down its back; it chatters contentedly, and then takes off again.

Earlier, I watched as lions played with lambs. (A lamb hid behind a tree and as a lion was walking past, jumped out at it. The king of beasts yelped in mock surprise, and was about to pretend to run when it discovered the identity of the culprit. No roar escaped its jaws; instead it licked the lamb on the forehead, and the two walked off together, the lion wagging its tail, the lamb trying to wag what little it had for a tail.)

I wish I could accept all this without the questions, one after the other, that keep hammering at me. . . .

I think back to when they first started. It was soon after my friend Lucifer was forced to leave Heaven, taking with him a third of all of the angels.

And the great dragon was cast out, that old serpent, called the Devil, which deceiveth the whole world: he was cast out into the earth, and his angels were cast out with him . . . And his tail drew the third part of the stars of heaven, and did cast them to the earth.

Those who remained were told that he had exalted himself too highly, that he proposed to be on a level with God and, in fact, eventually to assume His very throne.

How art thou fallen from heaven, O Lucifer, son of the morning! How art thou cut down to the ground, who didst weaken the nations! For thou hast said in thine heart, I will . . . exalt my throne above the stars of God . . . I will ascend above the heights of the clouds, I will be like the Most High.

I never was able to converse with him about this. The Casting Out happened so quickly. And since then I have asked myself, again and again, one singular question: What was the *whole* story?

As I remember the moments I did spend with Lucifer, I can see some elements of ego in him, some hint that he was different from the rest of us.

Different . . .

Indeed that was the case—the most glorious of all—with a countenance second only to the Trinity's. A majestic bearing, a power that made him truly stand out.

Others gathered around him. We all listened to his ideas. But as for myself I really never had anything to be discontented about. I yet recall my first moment of existence—from nothingness to awareness, looking up into the very face of God, knowing that though He had created ten thousand upon ten thousand of us, each was special to Him, each as though the only one. God reached down and took my wings and breathed into me the power of life, of flight, the reality of immortality. He first created my very self, and then He gave that self life everlasting.

I was grateful to Him. I came into existence in the midst of a place so beautiful, so good in every way that I had no reason to be discontent. When there is perfection, what could be better?

But Lucifer, I do admit, was not the same at all. Does this mean that God made a mistake? No, He created us—He never dominates us. We are His servants but not His slaves.

Yet was what Lucifer had done so serious, so pervasive that a loving, forgiving Creator could *not* forgive him? And yet later the Father sent His Son to die so that forgiveness was purchased for the rest of time. How could the same God not also forgive Lucifer and give His finest creation another chance, a chance to change, to—?

Always the same doubt—from just after the Casting Out to the birth of Christ as God Incarnate to His death, burial and resurrection and beyond, to the present. Doubt unchallenged, becoming ever more compelling . . .

Ultimately I decide I cannot endure my inner turmoil any longer. I shudder contemplating what I am about to do . . .

"Are you going to see Him now?" my friend and fellow angel Stedfast asks.

"Yes, I have requested a meeting and He has agreed."

"Do you think, really, that is wise, Darien? Why not just accept, and trust?"

"Can *you* . . . do that?"

"Oh, yes, Darien," Stedfast replies without hesitation. "It is not difficult for me. I see all that has been, and all that is, and what the prophecies promise will be, and I know that acceptance and trust are right and, yes, deserved by God as our response to all that He has done."

"I wish I could accept without question," I say, "as you are doing. I did once, before the Casting Out, but now—"

"Earth, my friend Darien, is where doubts grow. Heaven is where they are put to rest, forever."

Our conversation ends only because it is time for the meeting that will determine my destiny.

In an instant I am with Almighty God, alone, no one to interrupt us. He knew, totally, of my concerns. His plan had been set, I suspect, ever since the Casting Out, He waited only for me to ask . . .

"All around us is warfare, Darien. My prophet Daniel spoke of a ministering angel being late because of having to do battle in the heavenly realm. Satan tries to cause havoc whenever and wherever he can."

I had never been on the front lines myself. Suddenly the strangeness of that fact hits me hard. It is as though God knew I would not be a committed warrior but instead something of a pacifist, not at all certain of the enemy. Yet I had heard, in any event, stories about Lucifer, whispers from the battlefield about a shadowy, almost mythical figure—or at least that was what he had become over the ages as memories of him firsthand faded. The Lucifer I knew had a rich baritone voice and he used it to good effect as he persuaded angel after angel, but certainly he was not a loathsome adversary as would be told by returning warriors, with their tales of contending over the spirits of saints, awful encounters between demonic creatures and the heavenly defenders. I recall in particular an alleged foiling of a plan to storm the gates of Heaven itself; yes, it had brought chills to my very being, and yet I could never decide how much was battlefield bravado and how much was factual.

"I need you with me in this battle, Darien. But I cannot have you halfway. I must have your totality of commitment. You cannot fight an enemy whom you find appealing or whom you think is being dealt with unjustly."

God gives me a choice then: Indeed, I can go to Earth for as long as needed. Since time is not an actuality but merely a contrivance for the convenience of Man, I would be given the ability to go anywhere or any "time" I want. If I felt, at the conclusion, that Lucifer had been dealt with improperly or that perhaps he had reformed, then God would allow Lucifer back into Heaven, along with the others. If, however, the evidence supported the verdict, the justice of Lucifer's exile, then I would in fact return, alone, without so much as a whimper, and in the process forever abandon any notion of following in Lucifer's footsteps.

"Yours is a terrible responsibility, Darien. Your findings will affect all of us forever."

I leave God's immediate presence to ponder just a bit more what should be my course of action. Before that decision is made, I meet with several more of those in Heaven who had spent their mortal lives on earth.

One man tells me of being in an airplane, relaxing, when suddenly a bomb explodes. Directly ahead of him a six-year-old child is torn out of her mother's arms and sucked through a gaping hole in the side of the craft. An elderly woman has the fingers of one hand ripped off on jagged pieces of metal. The man chronicling this dies as he goes through a secondary hole that is just barely wide enough for him; he can feel flesh catching on the twisted metal and his lungs collapsing as the pressure changes drastically.

"It *is* violent down there," the man says but without fear any longer. After all, he is in Heaven where there is no fear, no sorrow.

I next meet a woman.

"I was attacked and killed while walking home," she says calmly. "It was at night. Perhaps I should have been more careful. But I tended to trust people, to think the best of them while not taking into consideration the sin nature that is part of every human being on the face of the earth.

"And, you know what, no one came to help me. I sensed there were people around, people who heard me scream, people who even could *see* what was going on, but they were afraid for themselves."

No bitterness exists—such would be out of place in Heaven. She is merely recalling the events. If anything, there was pity for the ones who stood by and did nothing, her dying agony buried in the corridors of their minds perhaps for the rest of their lives, like a haunting cloud always on the horizon.

"I left behind two sons and a daughter as well as my dear husband. I am so grateful that all of them do know Christ as Savior and Lord and they will be here, with me, eventually, and then there won't be any separations again, ever."

She is now smiling, a radiant look indeed.

I talk with others, find out more about life on Earth than I ever imagined could have been true, primarily because I had never asked questions before. My concerns, my doubts are spurring me on. Surely the picture being painted must be distorted in some way. How could it be entirely attributed to Lucifer? How could it be that Lucifer is guilty of stirring up such evil?

"Lord, I *will* go," I say finally.

He looks at me with an expression unfathomable but not unkind. My Lord could never be *that*.

"You go with the prayers of Heaven behind you," He says with great tenderness.

And then it happens. One minute I am in Heaven, the next, my odyssey has begun . . .

THERE IS NO TRANSITION PERIOD. *It is like stepping from one room to another. I go through an invisible door, and, suddenly, I am on Earth. I have experienced no bursts of light, no swirling gasses, no rolling thunder. I have instantaneously negotiated the void that must be faced by every human being, whether on the way to Heaven or to Hell; whatever the direction it is a journey, yea, destiny inescapable, profoundly inescapable. But I have simply gone in the opposite direction . . .*

It starts out well, this journey, for me. The day is Sunday. I hear the sound of hymns. I am out in the country. The sun is directly overhead, the air bright, clear. Flowers are blooming. I walk beside a busy road, automobiles passing by at a steady, fast clip. I begin to feel very good indeed. This is the way I pictured the world. Perhaps there are unpleasant things, things that should never be, and yet not to the extent we all had supposed. Those who went off to fight spiritual battles in heavenly places dealt with the extremes, the fallen angels who had gone over the edge and could never be redeemed. But they are the exceptions—all the old stories of corruption upon corruption simply cannot be true, I tell myself. *Nothing* could be as bad, as decadent, as pervasive as *that*.

And this Sunday, this cheerful, clear, mellow Sunday, goes a long way toward bearing out my notions. I see many people dressed well, smiling, walking up a pathway to the front door of a country church. It is a white building, made principally of wood, not a garish structure at all, but obviously one made with respect and love, for those who would worship inside and for the beloved God toward whom they would direct that worship.

I join the congregation. The hymn has ended, and there is now a sermon being delivered. The pastor is in his mid-fifties, tall, fine-looking, his voice commanding, encouraging at times, reprimanding at others, filled with the sort of wisdom that can come only from being based in the Word of God. It is a powerful sermon—yes, it talks of sin, it warns of becoming prisoners of the sin nature in each and every human being in that building—but it is a message of hope as well, hope that is the whole foundation beneath the death of Christ at Calvary. Otherwise, that death was wholly in vain, mocking His suffering.

The pastor finishes, another hymn is sung, and then everyone starts to leave. My attention focuses on one family in particular.

The father is still young, in his mid-forties, the mother in her late thirties; they have two children, a teenage daughter and a son in his very early twenties.

Happy.

That strikes me immediately. A solid, happy family. I join them as they drive home. I stay with them as they share a Sunday dinner of roast beef, natural dark gravy, French fried potatoes, green beans, and apple pie. (I almost wish I could know hunger so that such a meal could satisfy me.)

They talk quite a bit—I enjoy the sound of their voices. I enjoy seeing them laugh and hug one another, seeing them express what is wonderful, what is beautiful indeed about humanness. There is a bit of sadness in me as I see but do not participate, as I watch them sharing but must be set apart myself, with them but not of them.

Much time passes. For me, in Heaven, there was no such thing, of course. Time is nonexistent there—that which is forever cannot be measured by seconds or minutes or even millennia.

And yet I *am* in a world that exists on time, that can be tyrannized by it, that at the very least cannot escape it, all the smashed clocks, all the rundown batteries, all the rusty or clogged or spent movements notwithstanding. It is a world where the greatest of rulers, where the most powerful of nations, no matter what the circumstance, all are captive to time.

I shake myself from my musings. This family's day is ending but mine cannot. They sleep, but I am unable to do so. I spend my first night literally not knowing what to do. Others in Heaven, the humans who come in a steady stream, have talked of no longer needing sleep. For many sleeplessness had been a problem. They wanted to sleep, grabbing it in troubled scraps of minutes or hours but not enjoying the refreshment of, as they say, "a good night's sleep." Now, in Heaven, they do not have it at all and they do not *need* it. That seemed to be one of the more astonishing realities for so many.

While the family sleeps, I sit and ponder. They talked of pain, yes: an elderly family member is ill, in fact may be dying in a nearby hospital. The son is upset about his grades at college, from which he is home on vacation. The mother is concerned about her husband working overtime too much, exhausting himself. He himself seems to dislike one of his bosses but does not know what to do about it. The daughter is worried about a relationship with a boy at school.

But these are human problems. After Eden they became regular components of the human experience. They are everyday, commonplace, scarcely of significant trauma. The health of the grandmother seems the most urgent matter.

And they cope. They face everything with a spirit that enables them not to be *unduly* concerned, not to be paranoid, a word I have heard before, as I met with some in Heaven who were relieved that they no longer have any fears, anything *to* fear, their minds clear, free, soaring to the fullest imaginable potential.

I find myself becoming very close to this family, and it is odd that this is the case because whereas I can see them, they cannot see me; there is no interplay between us. As far as they are concerned, I do not exist. While they believe in my kind, they do not know about me.

So I am not prepared for the events to follow, events that will send me from that family out into a world I now wish I would never have confronted . . .

Within one week of the first time I encounter this family, they all are "dead." It is hard for me to think in those terms, for they are not now dead at all; and their present state of being provides that opportunity which could not have occurred in "life," that is, for us to meet at last. For that I rejoice. The wall finally has been broken down and—

But the *way* it occurred, the circumstances that took their earthly presence from them, translating them into spirit, as I am spirit . . .

That way is what appalls me as I think back upon it, as I remember *being* there and not able to do anything to help, an observer of human pain, trauma, looking and feeling but not—

During that week, wonderful, revealing, reassuring, I am constantly amazed by humanness. There is much, I suspect, that is unfortunately embodied in that word "humanness," but what I am seeing is a measure of what God meant from the beginning—love; patience; joy; a strength together that only the family unit can manage.

Moments of touching kindness . . .

The son, Jon Erik, asks if he can do the lawn for his father who has come home from his business especially weary, and really needing to spend the weekend resting.

"Hey, Dad, you look tired," Jon Erik remarks. "Take it easy for a change. Okay?"

The father, Gordon, smiles, nods, thanks his son.

Moments of a special kind of sharing between mother and daughter . . .

The daughter, Rebecca, is telling her mother about love, this young man at school whom she thinks she does indeed love.

The mother, Lillian, reminisces about her first date

with Gordon. They laugh together, Rebecca wondering if her friend is the one with whom she will spend the rest of her own life.

Moments cut short . . .

It happens as all four of them are coming home from a basketball game. Wesley, Rebecca's special one, played as part of the home team. He follows them in his car.

Night-time . . .

Another car speeds through a stop sign, hits the one carrying the family. It is spun around twice, then flips once and smashes into a telephone pole.

Instantly there are flames.

All of them but Jon Erik die upon impact. He manages to stumble from the wreckage, his body afire, his screams heard for some distance, I am sure.

Then he falls just inches from where I am standing. Scarcely a second later his spirit leaves his body. His mother, his father, his sister join him. They look at me, not knowing who I am.

"Can you help us?" the father asks. "We're very confused."

"Wesley!" Rebecca then asks. "Mom—what's happened to Wesley?"

It is then that they look upward. There is a light on them, engulfing them. Their concerns drain away. And then they are—gone.

Wesley tries to enter the flaming wreckage, but bystanders restrain him. He then falls into the arms of a stranger, sobbing.

Why?

They were Christians; they lived imperfect lives, but they tried very hard to please God. Everyone left behind who knew them would be asking the same question, and others related to it, over and over until the shock eases, and even the sad pull of this tragedy on their emotions disappears, and their own lives go on.

Wesley, as devoted as he was, as loyal and loving, and ready to spend the rest of his life with Rebecca, does recover. Not without struggle. Not without tossing in bed many nights afterward. Not without being so overcome with grief at the funeral that he has to be led away by his own family, for he cannot leave the cemetery of his own accord—there is, momentarily, no strength left in him.

He will think about Rebecca for a long time, perhaps to a greater or lesser extent for the rest of his life. He will think about her when he marries another, and they have children, and he wonders what the children of Rebecca and himself would have been like.

But someone else will pay, in a sense, a far worse price: the teenage boy, his system loaded up with drugs, who caused the accident.

He will be committed to an institution, and while there he will be gang-raped, and afterwards he will take his own life . . .

A little more of the world to which I have confined myself unfolds. With my human friends, with this family of whom I grew so fond, admiring them for their humanity, it seemed, at first, not so bad. Life for them had its sins, yes—impatience; anger; the threatening thread of lust between Rebecca and Wesley; moments that arose as a result of the warfare between flesh and spirit, and not to be excused, not to be brushed aside as acceptable because these were indeed *human*. All this, yes, but none so bad, it seems to me, as the blood on the hands of that teenage boy who killed them all.

I go to be alone, in a place away from humanity. I do not really know where it is. I think it might be a park. There is a pond in the middle, with goldfish swimming around in it, and a tall, carved-stone fountain and some pennies hopeful people have thrown there while making their wishes.

I am absolutely alone. It is early as yet, but the fact remains that I have seen none of what used to be my kind, none of those cast out onto Earth.

Where are you? I ask wordlessly. *I want to see you, to talk, to learn.*

Nothing.

Only the fish. Two robins and a sparrow on the grass. A squirrel scampering up a nearby tree. The sun is setting, darkness coming slowly, preceded by a golden light that reminds me just a bit of Heaven but then is gone, and just the artificial light of street lamps remaining.

I stay there—how can I judge the length of time when I have not as yet judged, really, truly, what time is?—and then leave, walking the night, not knowing where to go . . .

It is cold that evening. I see people—with their scarfs and ear muffs and hats—grimacing as they walk. I pass a theatre with questionable photographs displayed outside. Next to it is what the sign outside proclaims to be an adult book store.

I go inside.

I see the pornographic magazines and books, as well

as the so-called "marital aids." In the back are booths. And inside are men watching XXX-rated images . . .

I feel like shouting to them about their sin. I feel like grabbing them and shaking them, so repulsed am I by the very idea that a private act between husband and wife should be so degraded.

Am I upset over something minor? Am I overreacting to sexually starved individuals getting release?

No, no, a thousand nos if need be. Because I have been in Heaven. I have seen "life"—the only life, ultimately, that *is* life, not the temporary action of heart beating, lungs functioning, not that life which *must* end after a short time compared to eternity—life lived without lust, life that is pure, life in harmony with God's will.

I run from that place, its awful sounds, stale odors, and ugly yet pitiful sights.

I am shivering as I reach the outside. My whole self is shaking. And not just because of what is on sale inside the shop.

The implications . . .

Yes, the implications that spread far, far beyond that place on that street that cold winter evening.

IT IS MORNING.

If I were of flesh and blood, I could say perhaps that I had not slept all night. But not being such, I search for a spiritual equivalent, and find none except to realize that I feel something akin to tiredness. The shock of the events since I came to Earth is having its impact upon me without question.

A police car is stopped in front of a restaurant. There is some shouting. A man comes running outside. Two officers pursue him. They chase him for quite a distance on foot. Passersby jump to one side or the other. One is knocked down. Finally the officers corner the fugitive in an alley. He raises both hands over his head. I see them talking to the man.

"You realize that you have the right to remain silent," one officer says.

My attention wanders to the second officer. He is more distressed than the other.

"You are scum," he shouts. "How many kids have you destroyed because of the drugs you've sold them?"

"Hey, man, I gotta make a buck," the man says as he spits on the asphalt.

The second officer lunges at him and has to be restrained by his partner.

They take the man back to their car. I go with them, though, of course, they are unaware of this. The man is booked, as the expression goes, and put in jail.

I find out why the one officer is so disturbed. His son is in a hospital nearby, confined there because of a drug overdose. I listen as the officer and his partner are having coffee in a diner across the street from the police station.

"Tommy was going to be a computer programmer."

"You refer to him past tense. Is there something you haven't told me?"

"Yes, Dave, this morning—"

He breaks off the sentence, his face going red.

The other officer is quiet, waiting patiently.

Then . . .

"Tommy really had the ability to go all the way to the top—be another Bill Gates, the guy at Microsoft, who's become a millionaire several times over. Or that Steven Jobs at Apple. Tommy had their brains, once. But not any longer. It'll be a miracle if he can use an adding machine from now on."

"That bad?"

"Worse. His mind's nearly gone. As careful as Lisa

was! Giving up the cigarettes and drinking while she carried him, not even taking aspirin! And that was before all the reports proving the effect of that stuff on the unborn. We just used common sense. And Tommy was real, real healthy when he was born. A big baby! He weighed more than ten pounds. He felt so heavy to Lisa that we half thought there might be twins in her stomach.

"But now, oh, he'll 'recover.' He won't be a vegetable. But he also isn't going to be near what he could have been if that lousy—"

He bangs a fist on the countertop.

"I hate that guy and his kind so much I—I hope I can control myself when we come up against the next one. I just hope I don't go over the edge."

His partner pats him on the back, and they leave the diner.

Later, the officer—I find his name to be Henry—and his wife Lisa visit their son.

"Mom! Dad!" the teenager says as he greets them in his room at the hospital.

Lisa and Henry embrace him.

Later, the extent of the damage he has suffered is obvious. His words slur a number of times. He seems nervous, his cheeks twitching sporadically. And Tommy forgets a great deal—what day it is; the fact that his sister is due home from college soon; and he does not remember that the new hard disk drive for his computer had come in the mail, though his parents told him only the day before. And there is the frustration that gradually builds up, apparent in his manner, the quivering of his voice, the expression on his face.

Lisa and Henry know a truth that they have not as yet admitted to their son.

It will never be any different for him . . .

He is going to be the way he is for as long as he is alive, paying for his drugs for a lifetime. And his frustration will continue to build until, one day, he attempts suicide. He survives that attempt, but it is only symptomatic of other aspects of his drug involvement, aspects that will worsen as he gets older until, eventually, he goes on a rampage and kills a dozen people in a quick-food outlet.

Many squad cars are dispatched to the place. Tommy surrenders without a fight. One of the arresting officers is his own father.

Lisa and Henry say good-bye, not knowing, not having the slightest hint of what lies in store, and I am alone with Tommy. He paces the floor, anxiety causing him to perspire excessively, his hospital garb sticking to him. And then he lies down on the bed in his room, and starts weeping. Soon he falls into a fitful sleep, but even then there is no peace for him as a nightmare fills his mind with terrors that are not very far from the reality already experienced, and which will be repeated, even months later, as he endures the first of a series of drug-related "flashbacks."

At the age of twenty-six, Tommy will die in the electric chair. Not all the legal maneuvering conceivable—even considering the matter of drug damage—will do him any good. Only the date of execution is delayed, in fact prolonging his anguish. He spends more than four years in prison before that final day.

Time which does not exist is no hindrance to me and so I am there, in that chamber with him. The current is sent through him. His body jolts once, twice, then slumps forward. Tommy's spirit leaves that fleshly temple.

"You saw me die?" he asks as he sees me.

"Yes, Tommy, I did."

"Where am I going now?"

In the distance, or so it seems, I hear an eerie sound, like the gnashing of teeth.

Tommy hears it, too.

"I wish—" he starts to say, then is gone.

I feel, for a moment, a singular burst of heat.

And then an hysterical mother's cry that will never, never be forgotten . . .

THE EPIDEMIC HAS SPREAD
drastically. Riots are breaking out in a number of American cities. I witness one in Los Angeles. It comes in the midst of a so-called Gay Pride Day parade. (A revelation ranking with the most unnerving of my sojourn is how homosexuals can seriously use the word "pride," when in reality what they practice is intrinsically an abomination. I had never encountered the spirit of any practicing, unrepentant homosexual in Heaven. I did not meet everyone, of course, but at least I would have heard about it. I could imagine that Hell is crammed full of them. Whoever is not in Heaven *is* in Hell. It is one or the other for every human being ever to have lived in the past and any in the future. They

may not be able to admit this to themselves because none could escape utter madness if they did. But the question remains: How can they use the word "pride"?)

The so-called festivities begin at the Gay and Lesbian Community Services building nearby and continue on to Santa Monica Boulevard, a street famous for its hustlers lined up at the curb to flag down customers. Police make arrests from time to time to keep up appearances for the benefit of the politicians, but since the whole area is considered gay territory, there is a conscious decision by law enforcement officials to otherwise leave them alone, as long as they keep their soliciting to that one locale.

It is amazing to me that rampant perversion is not only tolerated but supported by the government through hundreds of thousands of tax dollars. Why are these people deserving of "community services"? Many of them will be shocked to find, on their deathbeds, that it will not be Almighty God reaching out to give them any of the services of Heaven. They will perhaps be even more shocked to find their homosexual behavior condemned so strongly by the Lord. But that is the truth, eternal, inescapable truth, however harsh it might seem to the unregenerate mind.

Not long ago, I heard someone say, "Did not the harlot about to be stoned receive the forgiveness of Jesus as He asked those without sin to cast the first stone?" Yes, He told her to "Go . . ." But that was not all He said. He added, "And sin no more." His forgiveness was coupled with the proviso that she give up the sin of prostitution. "But," I heard someone else ask, "Is not the forgiveness purchased at Calvary unconditional?" That it is most assuredly—but, on the other hand, is acceptance of

Christ as Savior and Lord truly from the very depths of an individual's spirit if that individual says, in effect, "Yes, Lord, I'll accept You as my Savior and Lord, but don't expect me to give up gayness"?

I watch the convertibles drive by, the flatbed trucks, the people walking in the middle of the street. Some seem, on the surface, quite happy, their faces painted brightly. Quite a number are lifting small bottles to their nostrils and drawing in deep breaths. Others are smoking what is obviously marijuana. A few are dressed in nothing but essentially the lower part of their underwear. There is an abandonment of inhibitions that they embellish with their garish look. Several are kissing not so much out of passion but as a pose for the TV cameras in evidence and, frankly, to shock those not accustomed to things of darkness being played out in the light.

I am amazed to realize that they seem to sense my presence. Several turn and glance and then look away. I suddenly understand why. Only the dying see me. And these people, these men with paint and garish dress, are dying, day by day, their insides . . .

Abruptly, the parade stops, as though the participants have been frozen. I feel the ground shake under me.

"An earthquake!" someone screams.

"No, it's a bomb!" another voice is heard.

Ahead, a column of smoke starts to rise from one of the buildings on the avenue.

A man, probably in his early twenties, comes running down the middle of the street. An arm is missing. He falls at the feet of one of the marchers. He raises the remaining one at the marcher, and shakes his hand, which is closed into a fist, then he falls face-forward on the asphalt.

As he dies, his spirit leaving his body, he approaches me, crying, "I hate them all—the lies, the degradation. My friends and I were free-basing, and it all blew up and—"

Gone.

As instantaneously as that.

The body remains but not his spirit. He has been claimed for eternity.

A riot starts, with people hitting, kicking, clawing one another. I remember a little vignette, minutes earlier. Two men were sitting in a park just off the same avenue. They were waiting for the parade to reach that location.

"It's a glorious day," the older one was saying. "We couldn't have done this a couple of decades ago."

The second man, this one bald and with a beard, was nodding in agreement.

"You're so right. There has been a lot of progress."

But somehow his voice carried no conviction with it; there was an emptiness around the edges. The more he talked, the more obvious it became.

Finally the bearded one broke down and cried, sobs wracking his body.

"I'm dying," he said, trembling.

"You—"

"Yes."

The older man pulled back. He had just had his face close to the other. His bearded companion noticed this sudden movement and looked accusingly at him.

"After all this time, you recoil."

The older man stood up, turned, ran. I noticed something on the lap of the other.

A Bible.

I could read the name on the tan cover, the name of a minister!

Pledged to upholding the Word and yet—

"Oh, God," he screamed. "Oh, God, how could You do this to me?"

He shook his fist at the sky. The Bible fell off and landed on the grass.

Tears streamed down the man's cheeks.

"It's—" he said, in terror, as he noticed a purplish mark on his hand.

He fell into a heap on the grass, his body shaking.

I approached him.

He looked up in astonishment.

"Am I—?" he started to ask.

"No," I interrupted. "You are still alive."

"But I will be dead soon?"

"Yes . . ."

"But why? Why in this manner?"

"You really have no conception?"

"No, I—"

He stopped. For a bit, the truth filtered through the canvas of lies which he had been draping about himself. A chill shuddered through his pale, slight frame.

Then—

"God made me this way."

"He did not."

"But I have been this way ever since I can remember."

He recounted some of his experiences. Finally I stopped him because it had become clear that he was not "always" that way but became hooked on the lifestyle, stage by stage, moment by moment, degradation by degradation.

"But I can't change," he protested.

"Do not accept those awful lies with which you have been brainwashed. Look at yourself. You are dying. And yet as you tell me what you have, you are not repentant at all but still fascinated, still hypnotized."

He started sobbing again.

"I can't change. It's too late. The big A—"

He got to his feet and ran. I shouted after him, but he did not stop.

the head downward
the legs upward
he tumbles into the bottomless
from whence he came

he has no more honour in his body
he bites no more bite of any short meal
he answers no greeting
and is not proud when being adored

the head downward
the legs upward
he tumbles into the bottomless
from whence he came

like a dish covered with hair
like a four-legged sucking chair
like a deaf ecotrunk
half full half empty

the head downward
the legs upward
he tumbles into the bottomless
from whence he came.

The sounds of the parade came to my ears, and I left that spot . . .

The riot has spent its fury. And the parade continues! I look at this with disbelieving eyes.

It means nothing to them. Just another experience.
The pain almost exhilarating.

I notice something around the corner of a building.
A shape.

Familiar. It's—

Another angel!

I am unable to move at first. He sees me, disappears. I go after him. Down an alley. Across a street.
And—

He slows, stops, turns, smiles.

D'Seaver!

A friend . . .

"Darien," he says, looking a little embarrassed.

"I thought I was the only one," I say honestly.

"You have just arrived?"

"Only a little while ago, really."

"What do you think of Earth?"

I fall silent.

"It *is* a shock, is it not?"

I nod.

"I mean, that it took so long."

"What do you mean?"

"You see how weak they are?"

"Yes . . ."

"It took so long to—"

D'Seaver interrupts himself, a strange expression on
his face.

"Let me show you a few, well, sights."

I agree to go with him.

First stop is a place with darkened corridors bor-
dered by tiny rooms, each with a single cot. And in the
walls between each room are holes.

"What is this, D'Seaver?" I ask.

Most of the doors are closed. I hear sounds. Groanings. A whimper occasionally. Someone cries out rather loudly.

There is a whiff of a chemical-like odor.

One of the doors is slightly ajar. I see a man with his body pressed up against a wall. His head is rolling from side to side. He is naked.

Corridor after corridor.

Men with towels wrapped around them but nothing else. Two in a whirlpool tub, holding one another.

The lighting is almost nonexistent. And in one room there is none at all. It is much bigger than the others. Several men are inside. They—

"D'Seaver, why are we here?"

"I wanted to show you."

"Show me what?"

"What is going on. To actually see and—and—"

"We must leave."

"But—"

"Now, D'Seaver, Now!"

We are gone. It is not difficult to leave. We just will ourselves to do so. We have no bodily substance as such. We can be anywhere we want, as soon as we want.

And we are in the midst of a cemetery.

"All of them will end up here so much sooner than necessary," I say. "Then, for all eternity, they will cry and scream in pain. They will plead for it to end, but it will not. And it will get worse. Every fear they ever had will be fulfilled. Every suffering they ever knew will be revisited upon them tenfold."

D'Seaver, only half-listening, points to something partially buried in the grass near one of the tombstones.

"That is a bottle of amyl nitrate."

"What is that?"

"They sniff it—the heart beats faster and faster—and enormous sexual desire is aroused."

"Why here?"

"I viewed the funeral. Most of the participants had brought such bottles with them. Two or three were talking about opening the coffin and making love, as they call it, to the corpse."

I can scarcely believe what I am being told.

"It is Sunday, according to Man's calendar, Darien. We should go to church."

I agree that we should. Not too far away is a modernistic-looking building. It seems to be constructed entirely of glass, almost in a pyramid shape except that the pinnacle is nearly flat. The sun shining off it makes the glass sparkle in a dozen different colors. People are lined up, waiting to be seated. Altogether there will be thousands inside by the time everyone sits down.

The interior is no less spectacular, with round metal beams crisscrossing the ceiling. Each pew is cushioned with a velvety material. In the middle of the altar area at the front is a huge cross, probably twenty feet tall. At the base, grouped around it, are bright red flowers. The altar seems to have been laid of marble, light-colored, with darker tan veins running through it.

All this is indeed impressive. Choral sounds come from the front, and a hundred men, women, and children sing as they file out and take their places.

Immediately I start to feel refreshed, as though I am about to take a bath to cleanse myself.

We stay in the back of the church. Minutes pass—it is indeed awkward for me to use such a term, awkward to think of anything at all like time.

The choir has finished. There are some announcements. My whole self rises in anticipation. I need this very much. I remember that first service, the family, all the rest.

The minister comes to the pulpit, smiles as he surveys the congregation.

"And, now, everybody turn and shake the hand of someone near you."

The people do this. A feeling of warmth diffuses throughout the hall.

The minister continues, "I want to introduce to you someone all of you have seen on television and in films."

A man with curly hair and a rather rugged face joins the minister. He talks about treating people properly, talks about caring for starving children, talks about being honest at income tax time.

A chill begins to nip me around the edges.

Finally the actor steps down, I think with considerable relief.

The minister beams at the congregation as he says, "There are good people in this world. They think in positive terms. They don't make negativity their god. They can control their own lives and make of those lives what *they* want. I think that's wonderful."

He pauses, then asks, "How many of you agree?"

Everyone claps. I do not. I turn to D'Seaver. He is clapping.

That chill is growing . . .

"And now—"

He holds up a porcelain angel. A nearby television camera zooms in on it.

"This is a gift to anyone who writes and sends in a love offering," he continues. "It is made of the finest porcelain, molded and painted by hand."

Then a collection is taken up. The minister leaves
the pulpit. A black man comes out and begins to sing. He
seems a little uncomfortable. And not because he is black.
But he does well, with more than a hint of real feeling as
he sings, "My Tribute: To God Be the Glory."

I hear someone in front of me whisper, "That's a
little heavy, isn't it."

Why? I want to shout. *Why is singing about the
shed blood of Christ so "heavy" for church? Why—?*

Several minutes later, the minister returns and begins his sermon.

I listen, with growing alarm, that chill totally envel-
oping me.

"The epidemic has been described by some as punishment from God. We all know that a loving God would
not do that. We all know that that sort of Victorian
thinking belongs with all that fire-and-brimstone talk
with which some men of the cloth try to frighten the rest
of us into submission."

He takes off his glasses, his expression serious.

"We make our own Hell right here on earth. We
make life hellish when we forget the principles of upbeat
thinking, when we allow negativism to crowd out the
positive, the cheerful. And what is Hell but *the most
negative concept of all.*"

I can remain no longer.

"We must not stay," I say to D'Seaver without turning to look at him. "We must—"

"Stop it, Darien. This man is good. He is just right,
in fact."

"Right about what?"

The minister continues: "My new book, which is an
international best-seller, is entitled A POSITIVE RE-

BIRTH; it has been made available in the church book-store for just $12.95, which is $2.00 discounted off the retail. It tackles what has been wrong with the church ever since Billy Sunday and Dwight L. Moody and others of that ilk thundered their protestations of perdition."

He moves with great flair, throwing his hands about, arching his back, his face a mask of exaggerated expressions. His voice raises or lowers with just the right emphasis.

"The time *is* here for a positive rebirth. Away with the gloom and doom!"

He holds up his book, waves it a couple of times before the television cameras.

"Place this book beside your Bible. Read them together. And you will receive a blessing beyond your wildest dreams. You will find your finances impacted very favorably. You can do better with God's Plan for Financial Enrichment than in any bank."

He takes some money from his pocket, shows it to everyone.

"Give to Him 10 percent or more of all that you earn, and He will return it severalfold. God is the best investment you can make. He does not want any of us to be poor. Remember that, my friends. And grab a little of the green for yourself!"

I remember a missionary I had met in Heaven. She had been quite poor during her final years of service. Gradually her support was being reduced by significant percentages. She went back to the United States, leaving the mission field forever. Her husband had died months before, and she was no longer able to handle the strain of the work alone. She got back to her hometown on a Saturday, stayed at a friend's house that night, and drove to church with her the next morning. As they walked up to the entrance, the missionary saw the minister park his car and then go inside the church. He had a new luxury model that cost nearly $25,000. She pulled her worn coat around her, asked the Lord to forgive her, turned around and never went inside that church again. In less than a month she was dead. The congregation sent some funeral flowers. But no one attended. There was a picnic that day by the Ladies Auxiliary, a fund-raiser to send the minister and his wife to Hawaii for a week.

No more, I say to myself. *No more in this place . . .*

"Now, D'Seaver, we go!" I say firmly, turning to face him.

It is no longer the D'Seaver that I had known. Something different . . . *something different.*

Demonic.

All pretense is over. No more posing as an angel of light . . .

Instantly D'Seaver and I are outside.

"Lucifer cannot know about you," I say, repulsed by him, barely able to look at what he has become.

His laughter is coarse.

He pounds his feet on the ground, cloven hooves moving with anger.

"You utter fool!" he shouts, slobber dripping out the corners of his mouth. "You act so surprised. You thought I took you to that place, with those men, to lament what they were doing. *That* is The Plan, Darien; *they* are part of it. So is that pompous fool. If he were any more transparent, he would not even *be* there!

"That parade. The riot. More that you may stumble upon while you are here, Darien. It is a real-life script. And it is being played out *exactly* as it should."

I turn and go. Behind me I hear the sound of shrieking laughter . . .

GO BACKWARD IN TIME, at first enjoying this ability as though it is a kind of toy, something for amusement. And that it is initially. To be able to see the building of the Pyramids! To be there at the American Revolution. To be present with the ancient Aztecs as their civilization was thriving, something that would have been highly coveted by modern archaeologists if it had been possible for them. It was a civilization filled with the worship of false gods, encrusted with heathen practices but undeniably grand in the sense of the knowledge possessed by the Aztecs, knowledge that amazed even twentieth-century scientists. So it was, as well, with the Incas and the Mayans, but even great knowledge, great power lasts, really, for just a season—whatever they knew, these brilliant peoples, more or less died with them, overgrown by the jungles out of which they had carved their cities. The kings and warriors worshipped and feared centuries ago now left only a legacy of ruins and the fascination of those entranced by questions probably unresolvable.

Backward in time, forward as well, through events and places that comprised the history of the Human Race, for good or naught. From the days of dinosaurs to the birth of the Industrial Age, to—

The Holocaust.

I am standing in the midst of Dachau, the German concentration camp.

The sky is overcast; at least that is what I assume until I see the sooty clouds of smoke coming from a giant stack not far away. Floating through the air, dropping down in patches here and there, are specks, thin, like burnt paper, settling on the ground, grey-white.

I walk down one "avenue" between two rows of buildings. Ahead a line of soldiers is standing single file. In front of them is a ditch, and standing just at the edge are a score or more of naked, emaciated men, their faces pale, gaunt.

The soldiers aim rifles, fire, and the men collapse into the ditch. Their bodies join others. This day is apparently being devoted to "thinning" the population of the camp.

"Garbage collection," I hear one of the soldiers say to another, his laughter hoarse, cold.

I want to reach out and throw him in the ditch with his victims. I want to call down all the wrath of Heaven and give him pain and suffering for eternity. And then I realize that that is exactly what he will have. That he and others like him as well as the ones *issuing* the orders will indeed have punishment never ending—it might not come in a year or even a decade, but it *would* come, inexorably.

I turn from that spot, toward the ovens. I see men and women tied, gagged, being put inside. I hear their terror. I feel their pain as flesh is seared by heat, seconds seeming endless and then—

Later, the ovens are emptied, bones not quite powdered put into bags and taken elsewhere. And then more bodies. An endless procession of bodies.

I enter one of the laboratories. A little boy, naked, is strapped to an operating table. A man, mustached, dressed in a white smock, is—cutting—him—open! No painkiller used—no gas to knock him out—nothing but the "live" operation, whatever it is, for whatever insane purpose.

Afterwards, I hear the "surgeon" talking to an assistant. This is all part of an experiment to see how much pain a human being can take before losing consciousness or dying. They do it again and again, to the young, the older, the elderly. Some of the old ones take it longer than do the young, but most die on the tables—there are a dozen or more of these in other rooms in that same building. A few, a bare handful, survive: some blinded when acid is poured into their pupils; missing arms, legs; parts of their bodies paralyzed because of their brains being poked around in; surviving, yes, surviving those moments of horror and, later, the continuing rigors of the rest of Dachau's daily routine, surviving to the moment of liberation by the Allies and beyond, to live the years left, few or many, in periodic anguish, the residue of being treated as they were . . . then death comes, an anticlimax for many, for they had "died" a long, long time before.

The ovens, the ditches, the "operating rooms" are part of what assaults me in an engulfing torrent. Many others die of disease or malnutrition; many commit suicide; some live with minds that have snapped so that, for them, there is never to be liberation, at least not on Earth.

I visit another camp, this one called Auschwitz. A woman is being brutalized by her "doctor." She falls into a heap on the floor. Her life is almost over. Her murderer stands over her, and she looks up at him, and whispers, "I forgive you . . . may God show you The Way," just before he slashes her throat.

In the blinking of an eye, her spirit has risen from her battered, torn body. She sees me, smiles.

"It is right, what I said?"

I nod.

"Good," she replies. "Is time for me There?"

I rejoice as I tell her that it is.

She is gone . . .

I go back to Dachau. Many years have passed. It is filled with well-dressed people. There are memorial plaques, with names listed on them. The tourists come and go. I wish I could shout to them, about all that had gone on before, a few decades earlier, the buildings, the ovens, the laboratories fairly ringing with the cries of the tormented, the dying.

I see a field next to the camp. It is lush, the grass brilliantly green, the soil dark, rich-looking, flowers vibrantly colored, trees healthy.

I wonder why. The rest of the area is so bleak. And

then I comprehend through a veil of revulsion that that healthy, colorful field, so serene on the surface, is where countless numbers of bodies had been buried, human fertilizer nourishing the growth of nature.

But cruelty was never confined to the Germans, I discover. The Japanese had their part in it: the relentless Bataan Death March was just one example. For the veterans who survived, it remains a harsh, awful memory. For me, back in time, it is current, palpable, a living reality.

Thousands are sick, wounded. They walk through mud. In other spots dust is so thick it clogs their nostrils and they cough, deep coughs that, for many, force open further already festering holes, cuts.

I see a soldier drive a bayonet through one of the prisoners, and then two other soldiers join him because the American is not as yet dead, and the three of them stick him again and again with sharp steel, laughing maniacally.

Some men die from previous wounds or malaria or other diseases, their bodies left by the road. (How many would be recovered, and shipped back home eventually? Not a large number, I suppose. They would simply rot where they fell.)

And once again I see something beautiful in the midst of it all, the march of horror that claimed so many lives. I see a man who is a chaplain on his knees, praying, as one of the soldiers hits him across the back of the head with a rifle butt. The chaplain falls but is not quite unconscious. This infuriates the soldier, and he is about to hit the man again, helpless in the mud. The chaplain looks up at him, smiles, and says, "Do what you must. I still will not hate you." And I see something utterly, literally incredible. (It is a word I hear often during my journeys, spouted carelessly, a word robbed of any real impact by its cavalier overuse but the only one that does apply, the only one to describe what I see.)

The Japanese soldier seems to understand what the chaplain has said. He hesitates, pulls back the rifle. And immediately I see a fallen angel beside him, whispering something into his ear. The soldier still resists. I recognize my former comrade to be D'Filer. I see D'Filer go to another soldier, and then this second soldier approaches the first. They get into a fight. The first soldier accidentally is run through by the bayonet as they struggle. He falls, clutching his stomach, just a few feet from the chaplain. The American crawls toward him. The second soldier orders him to stop. The chaplain refuses. The soldier aims his rifle. The chaplain reaches the body of the other soldier, puts his arm around it just as his head is blown open by the force, the nearness of the rifle that has been fired.

D'Filer is not pleased; he knows what has happened. He is infuriated by forgiveness. This is contrary to everything he wanted. There are two deaths, yes, but the result is forgiveness. He cannot stand that. He goes up and down the long line of American prisoners, driving the Japanese to outbursts of anger in order to vent his own. Prisoners are kicked, spat upon, clubbed with rifle butts, forced to walk faster when they can hardly walk at all . . .

It is now decades later, that same road, a monument being dedicated beside one section. There are scores of

Americans and Japanese. Some look warily at one another. But one American extends his hand to his Japanese counterpart. They shake, smile. The American takes something out of his pants pocket. So does the other. They laugh at this. One has a small Bible; so does the other.

"When?" the American asks.

"On my knees a year after Hiroshima. My wife and two children were caught up in the blast. They did not die immediately. They lingered for months. When I saw them, they were almost gone. They had been burned badly, their bodies flaking flesh. My children were both blind. They could hardly talk. I could not even hold them.

"I wanted to kill every American I saw. I wanted to destroy the entire country. And then I remembered Bataan, and the American chaplain I murdered, the dozens of other Americans I killed, beat, spat on, even starved. I remembered that that chaplain may have had a family also. And later, God opened my heart to be forgiven as well as to forgive. If I had never seen that chaplain, never saw him put his arm around Tanaka, and—and—"

He holds up the Bible as he wipes some tears from his eyes.

"This was the chaplain's. It is with me always."

A strange world, largely a kingdom of darkness, a place filled with the ranting and raving excesses of demonic hordes, former angels transplanted to a former Eden, cutting across it a swath of atrocity. And yet a world with such triumph as I had seen, such goodness as I had witnessed, such purity rising regenerated from a giant morass of murder, rape, unfettered passion, unmitigated depravity.

Being filled with all unrighteousness, fornication, wickedness, covetousness, maliciousness; full of envy, murder, debate, deceit, malignity; whisperers, backbiters, haters of God, despiteful, proud, boasters, inventors of evil things . . . Who knowing the judgment of God, that they which commit such things are worthy of death, not only do the same, but have pleasure in them that do them.

And still I could not find Lucifer. Had he been surrounded by a mutiny, and cast off ship, so to speak? If so, where was he? Where was the creature because of whom I had begun my quest in the first place?

APPROACH A SO-CALLED REST HOME for the elderly. It might better be called a dumping ground for rejects, mothers and fathers left there, like so much worn, excess baggage, to be cared for by hired professionals. An attempt has been made to make the circumstances as cheerful as possible, but for many it is a hopeless charade. Only one thing will lift the burden—the love of families that seem instead to have rejected them. This is the end of the road for the bulk of the people inside, a final prison, and a death sentence.

From the wonder of birth to the passion of youth, on to the achievement of middle age; and then the wrenching, awful waste of years spent as those in the rest home are spending theirs—a game of cards, an evening in front of a television and, occasionally, a letter from the family but coming like a single drop of water to someone in the midst of a desert; a walk on the grounds, a smile from a nurse, some food three times a day, and then to bed, the routine repeated and repeated and repeated until the monotony becomes a noose from which they feel their life is being choked out of them.

I see two women whose circumstances are as different from one another as could be imagined. Millie seems quite dynamic, spending much of her time helping the nurses with the other residents.

"They're my family," she says happily.

It turns out that they indeed are the *only* family she has. Her husband died of a heart attack a year or so before. Her daughter, son-in-law, and two grandchildren all perished in a plane crash months later.

"I was so alone it was ridiculous," she tells a new nurse. "But then I figured I had a Friend who would never let me down."

"Who was that?" the nurse asks.

"The Lord Jesus Christ. He's promised never to leave me nor forsake me. Though the whole world reject me, He never will. I have taken all my burdens and put them at His feet. And I am now serving Him more completely than ever before in my life."

She lives her faith, helping to feed Alzheimer's sufferers; those with senility dementia; those so crippled by arthritis that their hands seem more like twisted claws, the pain well-nigh unbearable.

"I can hardly think straight it's so bad, Millie," says one of them.

"Then I'll think for you," she says, smiling. "Let me start right now, dear one . . ."

So it goes, entering the lives of the others, laughing with them, getting them *to* laugh when instead just a bit earlier they had been crying, introducing the lonely to Christ.

And then there is Charlotte. Charlotte sits in her room most of the day, either in bed, or in a chair next to it. She eats a little, cries a lot, refuses to join with anyone in anything.

"Let me alone!" she screams. "Just get out of here. Let me alone to die."

Millie has tried to talk to her about Christ, but Charlotte refuses. Her room is a grave to her; she has already died and been buried in it. Death itself will seem at once anticlimactic to her. As far as she is concerned, life is over.

Two women: one with Christ, one without Him. One lonely, saddened, filled with self-pity, angry and bitter—the other vibrant, contributing, joyful.

"I wish I could do something to reach her," Millie says to a friend.

"Some people are happy in their misery," the other replies. "You are light; she is darkness. You draw people to you; she sends them away. That's just how it is, Millie. Thank God for those like you."

Millie smiles on the last day of her earthly life. I am by her side when her flesh-and-blood body becomes quiet, the heart and lungs still, the brain finally—

"Are you—?" she asks excitedly.

"Yes, Millie, I am."

"Am I in Heaven now? What about—?"

She smiles as she looks upward.

"Oh my!" she says an instant before she is gone.

I am at Millie's funeral. It is attended by a hundred or more men, women, and children. Many of those present had once stayed at the rest home, but Millie had revived their spirits so completely that the physical part of them also improved, and they could leave. The children had been brought to see grandmothers and grandfathers confined to the home, and Millie had mightily touched their lives as well. There are doctors attending, nurses, more. Millie's legacy of love would be remembered for a long time.

I return to the home. Charlotte is standing in the doorway to her room. She is holding a sheet of paper in her left hand, a note that reads: "I'm going to be with my Savior this day, dear Charlotte. Won't you take Him into your life before it is too late? Let me have the privilege of welcoming you into His Kingdom someday. I love you, dear one . . ."

Charlotte begins screaming, "How can she say she loves me? Nobody loves a mean old hag. Nobody!"

She starts toward Millie's room, sees the empty bed, the vacant closet, the dresser drawers all cleaned out, no toothbrushes in the bathroom, no—

"Millie!" she yells. "Oh, Millie!"

She falls onto the bed, sobbing. But she keeps the note clutched tightly in her hand. Opened on the bed, next to her, is Millie's Bible. She picks it up and starts reading a particularly pertinent verse.

If we confess our sins, He is faithful and just to forgive us our sins, and to cleanse us from all unrighteousness . . .

She had been harboring a whole catalogue of sins, letting her guilt over these eat away at her, turning her bitter, the bitterness manifested in angry and resentful behavior toward others.

She reads other verses dealing with God's forgiveness and cleansing. A few hours later she gets down on her knees and asks Christ to enter her very being and fill the void in her life.

In less than a week Charlotte will have died also. But before then she will have gone to everyone at the home and asked them to forgive her in much the same way as she had asked the Lord. Everyone is amazed at the difference in her.

Charlotte dies quietly. There is little pain. The peace of her death contrasts with the anger and the upset of much of the latter part of her life.

She closes her eyes, and stops breathing. In an instant, Charlotte's spirit, the real Charlotte, of course, sees me.

"Charlotte!" We both hear that voice as though across eternity itself.

"Yes, yes, I'll be right there, Millie."

She turns, winks at me.

"I'll never be rejected or alone again . . . will I?"

"Never."

"Forgiveness for all the meanness?"

"Yes."

She looks serene, a smile lighting up her face.

"Millie's got somebody standing by her side, His hand outstretched. Is that—?"

I need not answer.

As she goes, I hear, for a fleeting instant, the familiar sound of angels rejoicing . . .

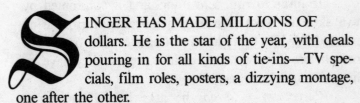INGER HAS MADE MILLIONS OF dollars. He is the star of the year, with deals pouring in for all kinds of tie-ins—TV specials, film roles, posters, a dizzying montage, one after the other.

But he cannot sleep at night—because a certain nightmare assaults, tearing open the darkness in bursts of wrenching anguish.

In the dream he is singing before a packed auditorium. The crowd has paid a total of $400,000 to see and hear him. He is at the top of his form, with lyrics that speak of a life of easy sex and growing demonic worship.

Drink the blood of the saints . . .

The words ride on electronic waves into the minds of the young.

Curse the god of your fathers; bow before the New Age Christ . . .

They hear, to leave that dark place and emulate in the soon-spent vigor of their youth, until madness comes on feet of crystal.

Stick your obscene finger into the face of the Almighty . . .

But something else happens in Singer's nightmare, altering in fantasy the outcome of reality. He hears a rattling sound throughout that place, louder, louder, drowning out his music. He stops, peers through the clouds of maryjane and hash, and sees light reflecting off an audience of skeletons. Some have flesh hanging like torn garments from rib cages, others have skulls cracked open, and a few, just a few, show stomachs with the tiny hands of babies grabbing bones like death row prison bars, yelling, yelling, yelling.

He turns to run, screaming, and is confronted by two skeletons backstage, bending over a mirror, using rolled dollar bills to try and snort up the white powder in rows before them, but they cannot because they have no lungs, no nasal passages, no—

Where am I to go? he asks himself in terror. *Where—?*

Behind him the audience is on bony feet, climbing up on the stage. In an instant he is surrounded, the foul odor of decay sweeping over him as—

Awake!

As before. Always the same. Turning on the light. A bodyguard rushing in. Sweat in buckets from head to foot.

And he will fall back to dream again, to scream awake as eventually the night is gone.

Over and over until—

He disappears one afternoon. No notes. No clues. Just gone.

Singer is found one month later, in a distant forest camp, tied to stakes in the ground, heavy ropes on his arms and legs. He has been partially dismembered. Nearby are his heart and his intestines on two altars of still-burning coals.

A diary is discovered; it has been mostly destroyed by flames.

One passage reads:

I found this group today. They seem so wonderful. They hate the whole lousy world as much as I do. Lucifer is their friend, and so am I . . .

He saw me, Singer did, as, earlier, his murderers carved him apart amid his unheeded pleas.

"I die from my own legacy," he said, "my lyrics my eulogy, is that it?"

"Yes, Singer, that is it."

There is a place for you, for me, where the neon emperor flashes his commands, and innocent blood is the wine of perdition . . .

As Hell sucked him in, across time and eternity, he sang, for an instant, of amazing grace too late . . . too dimly remembered from times of innocence since lost on compact discs and Dolby . . . before the encompassing abyss unending.

THE WANDERING ANGEL IS ALONE, on a vast plain. He stops briefly, looking up at the sky, sighing. *To go back there,* he says to himself, silent to the nothingness, shrugging wearily.

To go back—

He interrupts himself, a wave of laughter causing him to double over and fall to the parched earth, but with no reaction to his presence, nor would there be throughout the journey, indeed from the beginning of time, a mortal chill perhaps, a whisper of something there, then embarrassed silence, unbelief his scalpel.

How ironic, he remarks, again to himself. *I yearn to*

return to a place that I have spent all of history trying to convince the Human Race is indeed the stuff of myth, a phantom longing, somewhere that is nowhere because it does not exist.

He recalls the arguments, so profound, the thoughts planted as seeds, nourished and allowed to spring full-bloom, wreaking the havoc that atheism has been causing over the centuries.

The uniformity of natural causes in a closed system . . .

He repeats the concept with relish, savoring those words as though they were a gourmet meal perpetually spread before him, and he is being sustained by their nutrients.

A man is sitting in a chair in the middle of a room. He is alone. The chair is his point of integration in a world that is only the room around him. There is nothing beyond that room. There is no God, nothing but the three elements—the man, his chair, and that sparse, limited, very cold world.

"But there *is* more, of course," the angel says aloud to the desert and the sky and the distant horizon. "I fooled millions, yea, hundreds of millions. You all have labored your pathetic lifetimes not knowing that that is but one room in a vast universe of rooms and over it all is—"

He stops, looking around, shivering despite the noonday heat of that baked, arid place.

"Who am I?" you have asked in your agony. "You are machines, I say in return. You live in a barren world, beyond which there is nothing—just machines, that is all. You die as they do, turning to rust and decay and then utter, utter nothingness. The system is closed. God will not reach down into it, ever, because He is just a figment of your cowardly inability to face the reality of your despair."

Then he recalls the students.

"You were ripe fruit ready to pluck from life's tree. I put into your institutions of higher learning professors committed to humanism and nihilism and atheism. They took your minds as potter's clay, remolding and reshaping.

"I went into your churches and your museums and sang the melody of despair. Sometimes I disguised it with god words and sometimes I wrapped it in canvasses of Picasso and Gauguin and Cezanne and others, but it was there, sugarcoated as humanism and existentialism and situationalism. How words fooled you—how they midwifed your doom."

The angel sees the skeleton of a man, studies it for a moment, then goes past. Behind him there is no trail, no cloven hoof prints, the sand as ever.

"And this is your handiwork?" I say as we meet, again, an eternity after Heaven.

"Oh, yes, it is," he replies. "Hear the wind—it cries questions without answer. Look at the sand—hope and faith crumbled, through which we walk, undetected."

He casts a glance over the endless miles, parched, with skulls turning to powder, stirred up in patchy little clouds by not-distant cries in the air, wind from the forlorn lost.

"Man," he says without a smile.

"What you have made of him."

"Yes . . ."

And the wandering angel continues on, unable to turn back, past half-buried monuments, with rusty plaques of commemoration, and weapons of war now silent, the bloody stains wafted away, the sun mocking their decay. Toward the lake at the far horizon, its flames rising high.

I DECIDE TO SOAR. MY KIND HAS HAD that ability since the beginning. There was a time, before the Casting Out, that no limitations existed on our travels. We could go throughout the whole of what was, boundless distances, unimpeded, exploring the wonders of creation.

Oh, what a glorious period that was—Earth had not been created as yet. We soared from one end of the rest of creation to the other, saw the beginnings of life, saw so much that was thrilling and invigorating and—

And then a third of us were uprooted. One after the other left. We were given an explanation and everyone seemed to accept it but me, of course—and now here I am, soaring alone, above a world in the throes of such awful pain, pain of the mind, body and spirit so intense that it still seems almost unfathomable to me.

I see the millions in famine. I see babies with bellies bloated obscenely, the rest of their bodies bone-thin. They try to get nourishing milk from their mothers' breasts, but there is so little of that. And then they die, though not suddenly, not quickly at all, tiny rattling sounds of agony inside them, some twitching of the muscles, eyes rolling back, breathing in ragged gasps—for hours it is like this, not even to mention the slow draining away that precedes these final moments, a gradual death, worse than drowning, worse than a knife in the heart though, figuratively speaking, it is that as well.

And then the mother, in each case, holds her child, not willing to admit that her flesh and blood is gone. Her womb, a world in itself, protected him for nine months, but the outside world destroyed him.

I see one mother yet carrying a still, limp body hours after the child died—this one was three or four years old—and that body has become hard, one arm frozen in an extended gesture, the fingers stiff, wide apart. Eventually it is taken from her because already, in a desert land, it has begun to smell.

And then I stop in Alexandria, Egypt . . .

It is dirty there. Alexander the Great would be shocked by the place. Dirty is really too polite a word. Filthy comes closer, even though that seems still a bit mild somehow.

Yet I see many, many mothers in Alexandria who are apparently quite happy, tending to their children; feeding them, laughing with them, washing their faces, being with them in the time-honored way of mothers. The striking thing is that since they have known poverty

all their lives they have adjusted to it, and they are somehow content to a degree, literally because they have never
known anything else.

Children come up to well-dressed and -groomed for-
eigners, tugging at their sleeves, begging for money, smiling but not in a phony way, not in a flagrant sense of
trying to generate pity or compassion, not as a turned-
on/turned-off kind of thing, ready at a moment's notice.

They are covered with dirt smudges, their clothes
ragged, few with shoes on their feet, and yet a pittance
together with a smile, a shake of the hand, a pat on the
head makes them nearly ecstatic with joy.

I am now sitting at the base of the Great Pyramid
just outside Cairo, on one of the giant blocks, waiting
until sunrise. The scene is like the interior of a cocoon,
dormant, quiet, only the snorting of an occasional camel
discernible, the air rich with the pungent odors of a long-
dead antiquity.

The sunrise is rose-red, a flicker, then more, expanding light, the ancient city of Cairo first darkly outlined,
then aglow with light, then awash with it.

I see children again. This time they are with their
mothers, occasionally with their fathers as well, walking,
packs of whatever on their backs. Their bare feet stir up
clouds of dust with a reddish tinge, a texture like clay or
chalk, and the odor of tombs.

And I see a man with an old camel. They, too, work
the roads, confronting tourists eager to gain a little more
atmosphere. It is obvious, as I watch, that the man loves
this beast. They have been together many, many years. I
sense that neither has a home; they live in the open, as

countless numbers have done in Egypt ever since the days of the pharaohs, except perhaps for a small tent to help against the sweltering oven in which they find themselves during the noon hours of each day.

Undoubtedly, I imagine to myself, the man will die before the camel does. The animal will probably stand by his body, nudging him without comprehension. Someone else would take it on, and it might outlive the newer owner. But eventually, after decades of wandering, commanded by this man or that one, learning to depend upon each one, even to love each one after a fashion, it, too, would go to its knees one final time, as it did to receive a rider, grunting, and turn over, never arising again.

I cried because I had no shoes
Until I saw the man who had no feet.

I see such among the poor there in Egypt. I see a mother with no feet; she has her baby in some sort of bag hanging from around her neck; another child holds her hand as she alternately hops or crawls along. There is no man with her. She provides their only hope; they provide her only love, the center of her world. Though the poverty is there, suffocatingly, though often all she can give her baby is the milk from her breasts, she accepts, she goes on, she keeps that family of three together, with no washing machines to lighten her load, no hair dryers, no remote controlled garage door openers, no one-a-day vitamins or nail polish or other "necessities." For her, tomorrow will be another day just the same as today. She and they will survive until the day afterwards, perhaps another week or month or whatever the remaining span, not knowing what the day is or the week or the year, knowing nothing in fact but hunger and dirt and looking up at a stranger for a little spare change until—until the end comes, as it surely will soon, malnutrition and disease reaping a common tragedy.

I get the feeling, as the expression goes, that so long as they die together, so long as the mother can have her little ones around her, their bodies pressed to hers, so long as she does not have to worry about their love, unlike, ironically, mothers elsewhere, insulated from dirt and hunger and disease, cocooned in a world beyond the imagination of that trio on the outskirts of Cairo, who do not know whether their sons or daughters are alive or dead or dying, shot full of drugs, riddled with sexually transmitted diseases, crying out, alone, in some abandoned, ramshackle place, unlike such mothers, unlike such children, these three may die together as they live, with no one else but themselves, even humming some kind of tune to one another. I hear it from them now, mournful yet lyrical, made up as they go, music created from the very core of their beings—their voices a mutual melody of comfort until one by one the sounds die to a whisper and then silence altogether, except for the cries of the baby, until even that plaintive sound in the darkness, quickly dissipating, is gone, and the world goes on, ignorant of them ever . . .

There is hunger and disease elsewhere, stalking. On the fringes, laughing, I can see the figures of former comrades, gloating as the hungry occasionally resort to cannibalism. How could they? I must ask. How could they, knowing what goes down their throat, knowing what their teeth are tearing, their tongues are tasting?

It has happened before, I know. In my travels

through time, I learned, earlier, of the Donner Pass incident, a group of men, women and children, without food, freezing, taking this ghastly step to survive. Or that plane crash in the Andes Mountains, the survivors forced into the same grisly act of desperation.

This is a world once Eden. This is a United States once Puritan. This is a humanity once pure. No place is free of sin. It is only a matter of degrees. And who has committed the greater sin? Those who eat the flesh of others? Or those whose compassion has shrivelled and shrunken, a near-blasphemous mockery of charity, a selfish egocentricity like a wall around their hearts, causing the problem in the first place?

. . . only a matter of degrees.

The sin of no charity. The sin of cannibalism. Joined by a vast encyclopedic gathering of others. Sin in rampant poverty. Sin in pillowed, perfumed, pampered luxury. The same, a thread drawn through the gut of each living human being.

Many worship unreal gods; they do despicable things; their practices sicken one's very being. And yet they are ignorant. They have grown up in societies that know nothing else. I think of the Eskimos; they worship survival; it is their god; they worship It in the midst of the worst winters on Planet Earth. And when they live through another one, they feel that their prayers have been answered. The feeble old have no place; they cannot carry their own weight and do not contribute, so they are allowed to leave, no one stopping them, and they go out into the awful blizzards, and die.

The ancient Incas, Aztecs, and Mayans all had sacrifices of their infants, to appease their own gods. Some tribes in Africa consider cannibalism a "holy" honor. And many more, in the past and the present, in isolated places

and savage societies committing atrocity upon atrocity,
but with ignorance, with no idea whatever that that
which they do is a stench in the nostrils of a triune God.

How much worse for those aware? How much
worse for the chickenhawk, as he is called, who picks up a
teenage boy and they go to a motel room and the man
gets his pleasure by forcing the boy to abuse him through
countless demonic perversions? And demonic it is. Hovering grotesque beings—my former friends, my former
fellow wondrous creations of a God capable of creating
the majesty of what they once were, these very ones—I
know their names; I came into being the same instant
they did!—now propelling His other creation to abomi-
nable acts.

How much worse, I shout to the sky and the air and
the ground beneath me, to others once like me but now
laughing at my shock, my outrage, counting my loathing
as pleasure because they exist on such emotions, pain
their love, hatred their ecstasy, things whispered in darkness their beacon of light, blinding them, funerals their
celebrations, death their domain, Hell their Mecca, and
yet they are not satiated, their gluttonous appetites incapable of fulfillment, bloated though they are with the
carrion of their vile imaginings. . . . how much worse, I
say, regaining my composure, for those who allow what
they know to be so foul that the stench of it gags and
sickens and makes anyone with even a thread, a thin,
thin thread of righteousness vomit it up in gushers of
revulsion.

The next instant, my words a prophecy, I have
another glimpse, another layer of Man's sin nature pulled
back, revealing the blood and organs and marrow of itself . . .

THE RECEPTION ROOM IS RATHER spartan—white-painted walls, a dark tan carpet, a sofa, two chairs, a coffee table, and a single tall potted plant in one corner. There are no paintings, no plaques, just a no-nonsense "official" appearance. On the coffee table are some magazines.

Very businesslike, I say with no one to hear. The veneer of something quite ordinary, commonplace, yes, mainstream.

But beyond that facade is the opposite reality—a bizarre and grisly slaughterhouse. Oh, even there, attempts are made to seem institutional. Doctors and nurses are running about, some carrying clipboards holding charts, medical reports, whatever.

And it is large, this place beyond the reception area. Corridors spread out north, east, west. Each is lined with doors, dozens altogether, on either side. Behind some, women are undergoing abortions, with saline solution pumped into their uteruses; behind others, babies are being ripped out of wombs, limb by limb. I see a pile of arms and legs and other body parts, ready to be incinerated, and turn away in revulsion. In another, babies are in incubators, with nurses tending to them with great care.

I am puzzled. The nurturing of life side by side with the very destruction of it? That one room seems much like any hospital nursery except for the preponderance of incubators.

I overhear a meeting in an office that is rosewood panelled, with leather-covered chairs, and an enthusiastic chap sitting behind a large rosewood desk, facing three other men.

"It's been a wonderful situation, gentlemen," he tells them. "Our receipts have never been so high. This is the best year we've ever had, I can assure you."

"And there are suitable safeguards against any of this leaking out?" he is asked. "None of the mothers have any suspicion at all?"

The man behind the desk replies, "That's right. We have no fears, guys, no worries whatever."

What is he talking about? Angels cannot read minds, as God can, so I could not probe in his brain and find out in that manner.

What is—?

I do not have to wait long to find out.

I leave that office, and wander elsewhere in the building. Much of what I see is bloody. Some babies are still alive as they are pulled from their mothers, but most die seconds or minutes later. The ones surviving are taken to that same big nursery-like room. There is feverish activity as additional incubators are prepared.

"This is so terrible," says a nurse to another. "I don't know if I can continue."

"Me, too. It's ghastly. What if even one of the mothers finds out? They all think their babies are dead."

I pick up other comments as I stay in that place for a long while afterwards, compelled to know exactly what is going on.

Eventually everything jells. The aborted babies who survive are nursed to health and then given out for adoption. The mothers who decided to have the abortions are ignorant of what is happening. The black market operation prospers because they have a ready-made supply being created by the survivors of a million or more abortions annually. (Never mind what damage might have been done to a child, and which may not show up until months, perhaps years later. Couples driven to desperation to have a child, finding obstacle after obstacle to doing it legally, are ripe for such an operation. They have to pay a heavy price, but, for them, the cost is not the important factor. Being able to raise a child transcends everything else. And then, one day, they discover that this little dream of theirs made flesh will be retarded for the rest of his or her life due to the very techniques of abortion, a danger made that much more likely after a second or third abortion on the same mother, the walls of the womb progressively weaker each time. Retardation or leukemia or blindness or deafness—indeed, anything can happen—and no one pays more severely, no one faces more anguish, than the child and the adoptive parents. Those profiting do not, at least in the short term. They run with the money and have a good old time.)

What is supposedly not a living entity but a near-formless blob, surely not a murder victim in any way, what is expendable because it is not yet a person, like jello or a tumor or whatever, that is exactly what is making the perpetrators of this nightmare business quite wealthy, for they have a perfect situation, with no governmental records except that a baby has been aborted, and everyone knows that that is that!

I marvel at the genius of it, while at the same time I cringe at what this further reveals of the depravity of the times. It is a factory, an abortion factory on one level, and an illegal adoption ring on the other. But as awful, as sickening as that is, it is not the worst aspect of what is being practiced in that building. In yet another room, aborted babies, deformed or missing one or more limbs or blinded, are used instead of animals for various experiments.

"It's medically more accurate than using a mouse or a chimp," comments one of the doctors to a colleague who has been expressing some qualms. "As far as the mother is concerned, there is no child of hers alive. And the ones we are using would not be suitable for adoption. It's really a clean, orderly matter. Quite productive, I might say."

His colleague, a young man, nods finally in reluctant appreciation.

"You're right, I must admit. The women are having their abortions anyway, so we might as well turn what is, from their point of view, just dead meat, a memory they want to push into the back of their minds as soon as possible, into hard profit. Brilliant, I've got to admit."

They are chuckling now . . .

I can endure no more. Suddenly what I have seen and heard makes all the protestations about a "woman's right to choose" an even more pitiable distortion of morality, in that context, than ever. The choices of women everywhere are becoming the profit centers of a racket that has to rank with the most infamous in the history of Mankind.

I hear the sound of an explosion. The building is shaken; windows break; a table overturns; some plaster falls from the ceiling.

Abruptly someone yells, "A grenade! They threw a grenade through the front door."

Pandemonium erupts. Bottles containing arms and legs are knocked on the floor, shattering, their contents spilling out.

"Another one!" I hear. "No, two more. They're trying to kill us."

I see flames. A man runs in terror, falls, his white smock on fire. His spirit looks up at me as his body quickly becomes a charred mess.

"The fire was so awful, burning away my flesh. I couldn't stand—"

I say nothing.

"Surely that's not what will happen when—"

His expression is one of unspeakable terror as he disappears in thin air, screaming.

The nursery is untouched. The rest of the structure looks much like a bombed-out building during wartime. But the babies still alive are not harmed. Firemen approach, look with amazement at the sight. And in the days and weeks to follow, the revelations coming from their discovery will captivate the attention of media everywhere.

And what of those responsible for the destruction of the so-called clinic in the first place?

As difficult as it seems to comprehend, there is more outrage over what the attackers did than anything regarding the atrocities at the clinic. Somehow the real truth is muted, if not hidden altogether, for if it were to become widely known, the entire pro-choice movement would be severely damaged.

I "attend" a meeting involving a number of the movement's leaders.

"This could be a disaster."

"Agreed. We must do everything we can to stop the spread of the story. As it is now, we've got a reasonable-sounding explanation—namely, it's a humanitarian aspect of our movement. From time to time babies do live. What are we supposed to do? *Murder* them?"

"But *all* of them? There were so many, Gloria."

"I know, I know. But we've got to try. Too many years have been invested in what has been achieved to date. We haven't let truth stop us before."

How many infant cries must form a deafening roar from garbage cans and city dumps and incinerator refuse buckets before a morally and spiritually indifferent populace rises up and fights through the courts and, yes, as shocking as it may seem, any other means, including civil disobedience, that is necessary to stop a national scandal cold in its tracks? Where is the love of Christ in this? His love has nothing whatever to do with it, but His righteous anger, His intolerance of hypocrisy, His promise of judgment on those who would hurt the very least of His little ones—these have all the relevance necessary.

Reeling, I leave that meeting, wanting to get away from the stench that pervades it . . .

I investigate more of what goes on in other so-called clinics. None of the others seem to have such a racket going on. But then all of them, by doing what they are, find themselves in a grand delusion, a racket of a kind. They have allowed themselves to be seduced by the prevailing notion that a mother's civil rights are at issue— and the Constitution protects them on that score as well as the right to privacy and other considerations.

I am aghast at the specious reasoning people are capable of if it suits their goals. They ignore even the possibility of the agony caused the baby depending so completely on them. They brush aside the slightest chance that "it" is a "he" or a "she" just as surely as the mother herself is, only size and environment the differences. They choose personal convenience above the chance that they are no different than a murderer who takes a gun and shoots a storeowner to death while committing a robbery. When all the niceties, the distortions, the evasions are cut aside, the truth is seen nakedly real and unmistakable, namely, that there seems to be *not* a whisper of a difference between the death of a baby during an abortion, and a drunken driver running down a child crossing the street. Death is the result; the young are sent to their grave early.

And yet, on the other hand, a difference does become apparent—the child killed in an accident will never be forgotten, will be eulogized during a funeral, and given a burial, and there will be a headstone to mark the spot. The memory of moments of laughter and tenderness, of bright smiles and warm hugs and all the rest—these are a bittersweet legacy. But nothing of the kind for the aborted baby—the sooner forgotten, the better—pretend it never happened—throw the "evidence" away, like a rejected doll.

After visiting the final clinic, after being numbed by the vast carnage of human flesh dispatched in the abortuaries, I am ready to shout to God to take me back. But then I know He would not, for, later, the old doubts would return. He knew I would have to be actually confronted with Lucifer before my mind is ever made up.

In an alley adjacent to the clinic, in the midst of a large group of trash cans, I find a familiar sight.

Mifult.

One of my closest friends in the days when we shared many experiences in Heaven.

He is crouched down, in a corner. He looks up as I approach him. It is clear that he has been crying.

"I look awful, do I not?" he says, full of shame.

"Yes, you do," I reply truthfully.

"You have seen, in there?"

I nod.

"It's been a nightmare, Darien. You have no idea of what—I go through."

"Tell me . . ."

I sit down beside him.

"I am in charge, you know."

"Of what?"

"That—that! It is my assignment—to nurture the climate for that kind of slaughter, to get people to believe that it is acceptable behavior. D'Seaver, remember him, has helped me on occasion."

That chill—again . . .

"At first I tried to convince myself that there was a reason, that the arguments were valid. Deformed babies, unwanted babies, retarded babies. Why inflict them upon the world? Why inflict the world upon them? Kill them now to save them greater pain later. After all, they went to Heaven automatically. A little pain now, and then it is over. And they have an eternity ahead of them, an eternity of boundless joy."

He stands, starts to pace.

"It was easy at first, you know. The first few were uncomplicated. And then—"

He is visibly trembling, his whole being going through some kind of massive convulsion.

"And then I saw a baby scraped out of his mother's womb, piece by piece. First an arm, then a leg, then bits and pieces of the rest of him. Finally his head, the eyes still closed.

"Oh, Darien, I could hear what the doctor could not, what the nurse could not, what no human being ever, ever could. I could hear his spirit crying out. I could sense the agony he felt, his cries reaching up to Heaven, I know. He had been safe, warm, content. And then his world was literally ripped apart."

Mifult pauses, trying to keep his thoughts intelligible. It is a titanic struggle for him to do so.

"The next time a baby was born alive. The doctor tried to smother him, but that failed to work, though the baby was *nearly* dead at that point. In fact, the doctor thought he was, and threw him to one side, almost absent-mindedly. A couple of minutes later, the doctor turned, looked, saw the little body moving slightly. He then took the baby, broke its neck and threw it into a trash can bag. He—he—"

"Be still, my friend," I tell him. "Let us walk a bit. You can continue later."

Mifult agrees. We come upon an old man and a six-year-old girl. They are playing happily in a park.

"My next mission is to deal with ones like him," Mifult remarks. "We have established the precedent, and now we must carry it to the next step."

"Destroy the old?"

"Yes, Darien. Gas them; poison them; suffocate them."

My mind goes back to the encounter, earlier, at the concentration camp.

"They are as useless as the unborn child. They contribute nothing. They are sick and dying anyway. I must simply hasten their final moment here."

I stop, looking at my old friend.

"And, later, what about the retarded who are contributing nothing?"

His next words somehow seem more terrifying than all the rest.

"Yes . . . they are on the agenda."

We continue walking.

"This world was once different, you know. It was not generally realized, by mankind anyway, that when we were cast out, we found a perfect earth. We ruined it with our loathsome behavior. You see, Eden as such was over the entire earth, a place of transcendent, natural beauty. God started over after that, wiping the slate clean, and established the actual Garden of Eden, its physical, historical location a pocket reminder of what had once been throughout the earth.

"It was God's intention to expand outward after that, for man to have dominion with kindness and with every act honoring Him. But the spiritual battles continued, and when Adam and Eve fell from grace, when they committed the original sin, we all rejoiced with undisguised glee and abandon. We had reclaimed the earth; we had gained an important victory."

I had not realized this. But it makes sense. When

Adam and Eve sinned, they were thrown out of the Garden into a world gone from perfection to imperfection, from sinlessness to increasingly rampant corruption. They could never return to the Garden because it no longer existed!

Mifult points to a flower of special beauty.

"The world was once entirely like that ever so fine flower, Darien. And others like it bloomed over the whole earth. There were no deserts. No fires blackened vast acreage of forests. The air was absolutely pure. Any sort of death was unknown. There were no afflictions of pain, disease, unhappiness."

He stops, turns to me.

"*We* brought all that in, Darien. A gigantic, drowning wave of it. Again and again it battered the earth. It continues. There is no letup. Millions succumb. This is what *we* have wrought . . ."

We are approaching a cemetery.

"The bodies rot away and go back to the earth," he continues. "Families are torn apart, many for eternity. And all that is left on this one-time Eden are old pieces of marble or concrete."

He makes a sweeping gesture through the air.

"I have been a part of it all. I have helped with everything that is dank, and unholy, and loathsome. And I yearn to be clean, to look at myself and not turn away in disgust."

"Why have you not forsaken it all before now?" I ask.

"Because there was no one to help. I am surrounded by my own kind. I am trapped the way so many are trapped by their life-styles. You make the first move, and it is traumatic. Leaving Heaven to follow Lucifer was *that*. The rest happens act by act. If one stepped away from the others, he would not remain away. The pull is too strong. He cannot do it alone. So, he goes back, surrounding himself with others like him, cocooning himself in a closed world of those who feel his misery but likewise are weak. And it never, never changes—the blind leading the blind over the precipice."

He shudders again.

"But you are here now. You are not one of us. You—"

A child is coming toward him, with no adult near it. The child is crying. She goes past us, indeed through us, never knowing that we are there.

"Twenty million or more have never been allowed to live as that little girl is living. You saw what was going on back there. I am the one overseeing all that. Oh, look!"

The child's mother sees her, rushes up to her, scolds her daughter for wandering off.

"And there are the others who lived, who were molested, whose minds even more than their bodies were damaged often permanently by what *I* caused."

We stand in the middle of the cemetery. It stretches on for quite a distance in all directions.

"How much ground would be necessary if all the unborn I have destroyed were buried side by side? How many crosses? How much marble? Concrete?"

He sighs with great weariness.

"Darien, may I tell you about a dream, nay, a nightmare I have had for so long now it is impossible for me to trace when it began?"

"Yes," I indicate. "Tell me, please."

"I am very much alone on a plain. It is totally

barren—only sand as far as I can see. Suddenly I notice some specks at the horizon. They seem to be moving, though they are still too far away for me to be sure.

"I wait. Closer they come. I begin to see forms, of different sizes. Still closer, Darien. They are now near enough so that I can see what those forms are.

"Babies, and little children. Hordes of them. Almost like bees from a distant hive. There may be thousands, or more, forming a long line extending all the way from the horizon. They surround me.

"One of them approaches, holding out her hand. She says, 'Mister, why did you do those terrible things to me?' And I realize she has been the victim of a child molester.

"A boy comes up, his body covered with bruises. Others as well. Suddenly the crowd parts and I see the most devastating image of all: a tiny body, its arms and legs missing, somehow *rolling* toward me, crying, stopping at my feet. His head is turned toward me, the eyes pleading, the skin wrinkled and blotched and smelling, oh, Darien, smelling of saline solution. The first attempt had failed, so he was pulled apart limb by limb.

"I run, Darien. I run as fast as I can. Abruptly I fall and lose consciousness. I think I come to again, but I am not sure. Suddenly I feel someone tearing at me. There is intense pain. Then more pain. I scream out. But there is no response. I try desperately to fight against someone who is pulling at me, but I realize, I realize, I realize that I have no arms, no legs.

"The next instant I am at someone's feet. Looking up. Pleading. I have become that baby, Darien. *And—I— am—looking—up—at—myself!*"

I cannot say anything initially. What could I offer?

He was responsible for nurturing such horrors. He had on his hands the blood of countless millions.

We walk out of the cemetery, both of us silent. Down the street several blocks, a funeral is taking place. We enter the funeral home.

A minister is praising the deceased.

"He left behind a marvelous legacy. There are going to be people in Heaven because of his witness. There are families still together because of his wise counsel. There is less pain in the world because of him. There is love, more belief in Christ, more—"

The minister pauses, his emotions obvious.

". . . love," he finishes.

Others go to the front of the room. Their words are similar, equally sincere.

Mifult stands and hurries outside. I follow him.

"There will be no eulogies for me," he says. "I have not left love but hate. I have not sown joy but sorrow. I have not eased pain but caused it. There is no light as my legacy but darkness.

"I—I—I cannot stay with you any longer. I must go. The master is waiting, calling."

"But who—?" I start to ask, surprised.

Mifult stops, looking at me disbelievingly.

"You do not realize the truth, Darien?" he interrupts. "You are blind to the central *authority* behind all this?"

"But he could not be that—that—"

"Evil? You were going to say evil?"

"Yes—yes. Just because some of his followers happen to—"

"You fool! You utterly stupid fool! I can scarcely believe that you—"

Mifult suddenly looks terrified.

"I—I must go. Oh, no, please, I must go. I must go. I must go."

He continues to say those words until he disappears from sight, his voice lost . . .

But before he is completely gone, he turns. His countenance starts to change, much like D'Seaver's did, but there is a difference this time, at least for a split second, before his appearance assumes an identical malevolence, the difference of an angel whose expression is one of shame and fear and deep, deep regret, yet regret that is swept away by the habits, the behavior, the entrapment of unspeakable acts committed throughout the centuries of Man's history.

𝕴 AM AWAY FROM THE CITIES NOW, the soaring, the wars, the poverty. I am in the midst of a forest. I stand and smell the air. I listen to the sounds of life in trees, bushes, a nearby lake. I feel somewhat refreshed, and I wait, relaxing, getting my thoughts together.

Nowhere have I seen Lucifer. Only those who claim to follow him. Only those who claim that he dominates them so strongly, so inescapably, that they are bereft of a will of their own, submitting to him in everything.

If that is indeed the case, then how different from those who follow God, who have accepted His Son into their lives as Savior and Lord. Lucifer's followers, if they are to be believed, are automatons. But with Him, it is free will only, not an enslavement but a dedication, not an obsession but a devotion.

What an answer to the age-old question of why God *allows* certain things to happen. If Lucifer's fallen angels are to be—

If?

That question nags at me. Can the leader be blamed totally for what those with him do? What if all this is without his knowledge? If he has confidence in those who serve him, does he need to check their every move, approve each plan, detail? Perhaps his not doing so, if those in whom he has placed trust betray him, is cause for questioning his judgment in that very area of having chosen them in the first place. But that is another kind of weakness—hardly the same as Mifult overseeing the death of millions of helpless babies; the infamy of those perpetrating the Holocaust. Or—

My musings are interrupted by something carried on the air, it would seem.

The sound, far away, of a piccolo.

I stand, listening more closely.

Yes!

Rather like some of the music heard in Heaven . . .

But where?

I am attracted to it. Enchanted by the gentleness of the notes.

I find the player.

An old man, possibly well into his eighties. He is sitting on a flat rock beside a stream, the sound of the water a faint backdrop to the melody of his instrument.

I stand there, listening, awed by what I hear.

"Well, say something," he says, startling me.

"I—well—I mean—how—?" I stutter embarrassingly.

"You are not very secretive, you know. But then you probably thought you did not have to be. Is that it?"

"Yes, I suppose—"

He chuckles.

"I remember you from the old days. Kind of naive. A little gullible. But good-natured. A dreamer perhaps. But not foolishly so."

"Please, how can you—?"

"See you?"

"Yes? Tell me how."

"Because I came along with them, for the ride. I am the only one who did, of course. The others were quite zealous from the beginning. For me, it was just a matter of curiosity. Though I, too, was cast out, guilt by association, I guess you might say, I have never really joined the others. I have remained uncommitted to their atrocities. But I can never return, either, to the way it once was. God asked for a choice. I made mine, however half-heartedly, and with motives that were substantially different, but it was made just the same. And I am stuck with the consequences, unfortunately."

There is a note of wistfulness in the way he speaks. Underlined by a profound sadness.

"I have counterparts among the human beings of this world, you know. People who want to go along for the ride, who are faintly attracted by the bravado of many of their contemporaries, but torn by the knowledge that they cannot serve two masters—allowing themselves to be beckoned by the one, they end up rejecting the other."

I stand there, still amazed.

"But that old man's body which you inhabit? How?"

"He is the same way. He is unaware, of course, that we are here. He will die soon, and then I must find someone else. It is the same with the others, at least the ones who have been assigned the possessions—they work from within while the rest wreak havoc from without, oppressing with equal vengeance."

"You have been in—inside others?"

"When I choose to be. I have not succumbed to any orders by anyone. I do as I wish."

He pauses, very briefly, then talks with affection about the old hands that are writing down his thoughts, hands mottled with the spots of a liver in distress, varicose veins apparent, nails turning faint yellow.

"I started a journal some time ago. Here it is. See, he's writing in it now."

"And it will be passed on to someone else when you move on?"

"Exactly. There will be new editions when each of the old starts to crumble."

"But why?"

"I am known as Observer. It is what I do."

"But who is going to read it?"

"Those who play host to me. They read it. But they see it only as a collection of myths. They read, oh, yes, they do that, but their understanding is darkened—and, eventually, each will put it aside."

I am eager to know the contents of that book.

"It is to be read only when it is to be read," Observer says ambiguously. "It is a perpetual legacy, left behind by a wandering spirit hoping that, someday, those who have it will indeed comprehend."

I want to pursue this matter further with him, but I know that I will not be at all successful. Instead I content myself with the bits and pieces told to me by Observer as we sit there by that stream, the sun poking through overhead branches, and glistening off the rippling water.

"I have seen The Fall and The Flood. I have been with John on Patmos, at the French Revolution, the Civil

War, the two World Wars—from the ancient days to the computer age. And, you know, even I feel something akin to weariness."

He hesitates, then: "You have been around also, have you not?"

I nod.

"But there is a difference between us, my former fellow inhabitant of Heaven. You have sampled history; I have been through it. You have dabbled here and there—I have experienced centuries *as* centuries. In Heaven, time was an impossibility. For Man, it is a necessity. And to a great extent we—the others and I—are entrapped by many of the constraints, the conventions, the limitations of the very creature they—not me, please understand, *never* me—would like to destroy, would like to snatch from the loving arms of a kind and generous Creator."

He begins to sob then.

"I do this often. These are not tears, of course—we are beings of spirit, not tear ducts and blood and nerve endings. But we cry spiritually. We cry with emotion and depth even more profoundly than this old man who wept many years ago over the death of his wife."

Observer/old man stands, walks to a deeper, broader part of the stream, points to some fish there.

"Many will not make it, you know. They will die in that stream or be hooked by fishermen and fried in a skillet and eaten with delight. But they do not know the future. The others and I do. That is why they are so frenzied. That future is always closer, never forestalled. For these fish, it may be the frying pan—for us, it *is* the fire."

He shakes himself with great weariness.

"I cry because I know I am doomed. I know what is in store. I will be there in the lake of torment with all the rest. It is the choice each being makes—of spirit or of flesh—and there by it he must abide for all eternity, in pain or—or in peace."

He turns, sits down again, age readily apparent.

"My host is dying," Observer says simply. "He will see us soon."

The pen drops from the old man's hand as he clutches his chest. The ancient book falls to the ground, amongst some autumn leaves. Lips issue a single cry and then are frozen together, eyelids closed, head bent to one side.

First it is Observer as spirit en toto who leaves that body, and I see an angel much like myself but also very different, wings at half-mast, face pale, the glow of Heaven gone, his lostness apparent in the tragedy of separation from God mirrored in his eyes, the forlornness of his very countenance. And then the old man's spirit, that which is him in actuality, not the disposable cloak soon to rot away, also leaves that fleshly shell.

"You've been with me many years, have you not?" he asks, looking at Observer.

Observer agrees that this has been so.

"I was a good man, kind, charitable."

Observer nods.

"I never engaged in adultery. I lied little."

"That is correct."

"I never cursed any man. I never stole money. I am good, am I not?"

"Yes, you are."

He smiles, but it fades as quickly.

"But why are *they* waiting for me?"

In the surrounding forest are a dozen fallen angels. The sight of them is chilling.

"I have helped the homeless, fed the starving, comforted the dying."

The dozen shapes are beckoning, cloven feet stamping the ground.

"I have served on church committees, raised money for missionaries. I have also planned picnics for the elderly and—and—"

The shapes move from the trees into the clearing.

"Must they have me? Must all my good be as nothing?"

They grab him and take him away, his screams filling the air. One turns, smiles momentarily at Observer. And then is gone with the others.

Observer is shaken.

"I must wait here until the body is found," Observer notes, his voice trembling. "It may not be long. It will be found, along with the book, and I will go along until it passes into the hands of someone else like me, and whoever that is will provide me with pen, ink, and a hand to write. I am called Observer, yes, but I have felt that another appellation was perhaps a trifle more accurate."

"And what would that be?"

He grimaces with centuries of awareness, centuries that weigh upon him like some kind of boulder, pressing him down, sapping away his vitality.

I can scarcely hear him at first, and tell him so. Then he speaks louder as he says, "TuMasters, that is what it should be, would you not agree?" Mifult. D'Seaver. D'Filer. And now TuMasters. What a motley crew, the bane of humanity. And yet there are more, of course, out there among the masses, planting, nurturing, reaping.

"I live under a delusion, you know, as all of us do.

Many of the others abort, rape, slaughter. I seem so bland in comparison. I seem to do nothing but observe, hence my title. And that is the appalling reality of my existence. I look; I write down my useless insights through my hapless hosts; but that is all. I interfere not. I stay within a limited circle, insulated, my hosts and I. And we let the world collapse around us."

He has been looking up at the sky, which has but a lone cloud at that time and place.

"When you get back, please, please, please tell Him how very sorry I am."

I start to speak, to say something very evangelical, if you will, to tell him it is not too late.

But he has turned his back on me, and he is sitting by that old, old book, the piccolo lying nearby, and the moment of regret has passed, the door to himself is closed, and Observer will do as he has always done . . .

THE KITTEN IS MEWING.
It cannot be more than a few weeks old, the fur still tufted with something like fuzz. A man in a white smock is holding it in his right hand. With his left he is putting little beads of fluid from a dropper into each of its eyes.

The kitten cries louder. The man puts it in a cage with another of its kind, then leaves.

The first kitten cannot stand. Little knives of agony slice continually from its eyes into its brain and then throughout its tiny body. It tries to wash the awfulness away by licking its paw and then rubbing that paw over its left eye, and next the other paw over the right eye. Yet this is to no avail. The pain continues. In fact, it is getting worse.

The kitten starts to vomit, what little food was held in its young stomach spewing onto the newspaper underneath, onto its own fur, and that of its companion.

The kitten can no longer see, its blindness caused by an acid-based dye that has literally eaten away much of the soft material of its eyeballs.

Its body shakes once, twice, its limbs extended out straight as though frozen in that position. Then it gasps up some blood. And dies.

Its companion walks hesitantly over to the still form, not aware of what has happened, and lies next to it, hoping to comfort what is now beyond that.

A short while later the man in the white smock returns, finds the lifeless body, dumps it into a nearby wastebasket, takes the second kitten, and another dropper with a different solution inside and—

Madison Avenue.

Product marketing meeting.

A tall man, his shirt sleeves rolled up, shows a chart to others in the room.

"It's a great new color," he beams. "I'm calling it luminescent pearl. The women will love it."

The chimpanzee cannot stop scratching its head. It has been doing so for nearly an hour. Its fingertips are bloody, pieces of skin hanging from—

"Last year our best shade was sunset orange," the man continues.

The chimp has blood all over its head, but still it keeps scratching. It does not know what else to do.

"How many units do we expect to sell?" He repeats the question that has just been asked.

He inputs some figures on a calculator in front of him and gives the result to those in the conference room with him.

"That's pretty good, if it's accurate," someone speaks up.

There is general agreement that the outlook certainly is appealing, the more dollars the better.

The chimp is covered with his own blood, for it has continued to scratch itself, tearing more and more flesh. Now too weak to do anything else, it slumps back across one side of the cage.

"How about the testing?" a little man on the left side of the oak conference room asks. "What about the safety factor?"

"No problem at all," the main speaker replies. "We're finalizing the results now. You know what I always say? Better to kill a chimp than to harm one single hair on a single customer's head. We can always find another chimp, but finding customers isn't always easy."

It moans with enormous anguish several times, then is silent altogether, its eyes rolling upward in its sockets, slobber dripping out of its mouth and down its chin, hanging like dewdrops from the black hairs. And then it dies.

Everyone claps. The mood is buoyant. They have a new color. And sales have never been better.

I am privy to more in other panelled conference rooms in tall buildings along that avenue. Other products are being generated. More dollars coveted. More suffering generated for animals at the mercy of those whose highest ambition, whose most compelling ideal, is additional profit for their companies.

"Who cares if they need it?"

"That's right. We'll create the desire and masquerade it as need."

All the demographics are there. All the convincing marketing research designed to lull the public into an acceptance of whatever the manufacturers care to purvey.

This is not America, I cry out to unheeding ears. It is not the vision of the Pilgrims or the Puritans. They left one kind of domination but not to sow the seeds of another in its place.

And flashing across my vision is a montage of faces, the faces of mothers whose babies are deformed because of cigarettes. Or alcohol. Or drugs innocently taken in trust of a doctor's prescription, only to see a pitiful, twisted little shape coming from the womb, and turning for solace only to hear the shouts of "Abort! Abort! Abort!" all around. You should have killed the thing. You should have—

They are out there in the cities, the towns, the villages. Pumping poison into their systems, through mouths and skin pores and into veins. Poison over the counter, in the midst of shopping malls. Or in a secluded place from a man who profits, chuckling at his fruits. Poison into the temple made by God, graffiti of the spirit, but far more deadly than initials or obscenities or protests on an outdoor wall.

Poison, yes, packaged and labelled and advertised. Poison to color the hair. Poison to prolong the "freshness" of food. Poison to move the bowels. Tested, oh, yes, they test all of it. They reap their profits on the backs of God's helpless ones, the dogs and cats and birds and mice and monkeys and other creatures who wait in their cages for the inevitable, condemned not for crime but commerce.

Present your bodies a living sacrifice . . .

But is a body riddled with the residue of mindless

consumption, consumption ignorant of the content of
what is being consumed, dictated even among His chosen
ones by the latest "discovery" to retard aging, change hair
color, take away bad breath, ban body odor, bring on
sleep, calm frazzled nerves during the day, give a reason
for smiling, is such a body cosmeticized, aromatized,
plasticized, artificialized for profit and not a dedication to
the betterment of the Human Race, is such a body trau-
matized by the media, pummelled by sensation at every
turn, is such a body indeed truly, truly, truly a living
sacrifice or rather a kind of mannequin, dressed up, pret-
tied up, propped up by the merchandising to which it has
succumbed? Is there not in that Scriptural admonition at
least the implication that those bodies are to be worthy as
well as living? Is a gift to a charity of a suit with holes and
patches and loose threads and stains and rips in fact a
gift? Or, dare I say, an insult instead? Too often, as I have
seen in my travels across Earth, a gift is not actually that
but instead more like a spent whore, riddled with disease,
crippled by exhausted inner drives, drained of energy,
worthless in her profession, lying down before God and
saying, "Here I am, Lord." That body of that whore has
already been sacrificed, but not to God. When a celebrity
leaves the glittery world of show business and professes
salvation by faith in Christ, is it plus nothing and is it
worthy? Or has an illusion been created, the formula now
salvation by faith in Christ plus transcendent media attention that revives a slumping career?

But this is the world. The domain of the flesh. What
about the get-rich-quick minister steering his congregation on the road to prosperity? Offering them keys to a
generously filled bank vault instead of Heaven? The heal-
er on television who claims the name of Christ and then

makes a sideshow of purported healing that even the most naive, the most gullible find patently absurd? What about the "Jesus loves me" Ping-Pong paddle peddlers? Those who take sacred verses dealing with Christ being the Light of the World and make that Scriptural truth instead a Jesus night-light to be used in bedrooms everywhere? What about all the rest of holy hardwaredom? Pens and bracelets and bookends and handkerchiefs and endless other products made "righteous" by the name of Christ?

Oh, God, I say, and not in vain—I could never use my Creator's name in vain—this is what has become of America, the world? This is His creation, now, a little higher than the angels? This is Earth, once Eden?

If I had a stomach, if there were bowels within me, I would be in great distress. I would vomit up the sickness that grips me, the slop from within like that which I see without, nauseating and vile.

And even now, yet another wretched truth unravelling, I still see not the creature accused of it all, only those called demons, spirits of the hideous and profane, things that bump in the night, and—

Lucifer.

Not in the abortion mills. Not in the Madison Avenue conference rooms. Not in the gay parties of Hollywood.

Emissaries aplenty, but not Lucifer, my former fellow inhabitant of heavenly places.

Where are you, son of the morning?

WHERE AM I TO GO?

I cannot be seen except by dying human beings on the way to Heaven or Hell. I am as close to desperation as I can possibly be, my inner turmoil so strong that I feel moved to petition to Him to let me back, that I do not really need to find out the truth about Satan because I perceive the truth about the world to which he has been confined for so long. But I suspect God would not allow me to return to His Kingdom under such conditions because, in His wisdom, He knows the old doubts would crop up again later, and—

An idea springs into my mind. If I can just not give up in trying to locate Lucifer, perhaps, upon doing so, I could alert him to what is going on, and together we could make things right. What a triumph *that* would be! And the return of the highest archangel to Heaven would surely be an event of rejoicing without precedent. If we all used to celebrate over the salvation of one sinning human being, what would it be like if Lucifer returned in contrition and with the banishment of all the evil in the world as his legacy?

The possibilities overwhelm me. And I become more deeply committed than ever to the goal of finding Lucifer, for the new reason makes a pygmy of my previous one. Lucifer and I allies! Banishing the perversion, the drugs, the abortions, banishing all the other corruptions that have swept over Earth like the most epochal tidal wave of history.

I ask fallen angel after fallen angel. As before, it is not difficult to find them. A whole horde are at a heavy metal rock concert, infiltrating the audience, backstage with the strange-garbed musicians, and—

No one will tell me. The most I can get out of them is that Lucifer will find me, not the other way around, when he wishes to do so.

I discover my former comrades at a television station during a debate between a minister who claims that the Bible *contains* God's truth, and another who protests that the Bible *is* His truth, from cover to cover. And they also are in the newscaster's booth as he tells a "neutral" story about the Communist takeover of another country in Central America. And they are there as commercials are being telecast, commercials that appeal to the vanity of millions of viewers. They are everywhere at that station, in every department, because this is where their lies, their distortions can be disseminated to a wider number than even they could reach otherwise. But all profess ignorance about where Lucifer is, although at the very mention of his name, they become exceedingly nervous, paranoid.

One in particular seems more upset than the others. His name is Nufears.

"Why do you want to meet Lucifer?" he asks. "Why would anyone?"

He looks from side to side, apprehension growing.

"He is not what you may be expecting."

"But I have to see for myself."

"I must tell you that he—"

He disappears, suddenly, without explanation.

I stand there in a corridor, rock music and interviews and newscasts being spun out all around me. And I am just as puzzled as ever.

More time passes. At different places. In that city. And in others. And I am now in a place where it could be expected that I would find the highest concentration of fallen angels anywhere in America, surpassing even the number in Hollywood.

The President is dying. Gathered around him are his family, two physicians, and three Cabinet members. The rigors of office have taken their toll on the oldest President in the history of the United States.

"He should rest now," a doctor says softly, and they all leave the room.

The First Lady, as though sensing that he will be gone when she returns, whispers, "Good-bye, my love . . ."

The President knows of my presence, so close to death is he by then, and seems not startled by it.

"Almost the moment?" he asks, his voice hardly audible.

"Yes, Mr. President, it is."

"Oh, how I rejoice over that. How I indeed rejoice."

"You have done well these seven years."

"I tried very hard, you know. I witnessed to as many members of Congress, foreign heads of state, and whoever else I could. Many paid no heed, but I hope I managed to reach a few."

"In Heaven there is great anticipation over your imminent arrival."

"Is that really, really the case, my new angel friend?"

"Oh, yes. The President who tried to govern in the *right* way even though that did not guarantee how correct he was from a *political* point of view. You put God first always, and nothing else matters in the long run."

"And I know how much of a miracle it was that I was reelected!"

He coughs, then says: "I once heard a joke. St. Peter welcomes a minister and a politician through the so-called pearly gates. The former is assigned a very nice place to live in for eternity but not especially elaborate. The latter is given a palace, a stunning residence indeed. The politician is appreciative but puzzled. He asks St. Peter, 'But why am I being blessed so mightily while a man of the cloth is treated so humbly?' St. Peter replies, 'It is not uncommon for ministers to come here and stay forever. But it is a momentous event indeed when that happens to a politician!' "

I laugh at the joke, then say, "You must have been perplexed by a great deal of what you have seen, here, over the years."

"Oh, a considerable amount has been ghastly. If ever there was a capital as much for the Devil as for the nation, then Washington, D. C., is it, I am afraid to say."

"Terribly frustrating for you, Mr. President?"

"More than anyone except God Himself will ever know. For example: If I could have established an AIDS quarantine, I would have. It seems suicidal not to have done so. In virtually all other periods of epidemic throughout history, from ancient times to the modern, quarantines have been accepted as a necessity, and this one has perhaps the most devastating potential of all. But certain segments of our society got wind of it, labelled it as a transgression against their civil rights, and, well, as it turned out, they enlisted their cohorts in the media and in the judicial system and I soon had the columnists, the commentators, the judges, and the ACLU against me from the beginning. How blind we have become in this generation. Civil rights my foot! It's a matter of morality and the public health!"

"They would find Heaven a very quarantined place, in one sense," I say in agreement. "No one is an idolater, effeminate, whoremonger, sorcerer . . ."

"How well I know that verse, how much it and others like it have guided me over the past seven years. The threats I received, many of them in the most obscene terms! That kind of reaction only strengthened my determination, I can assure you.

"In addition, I wanted to get prayer back in schools, but I was ridiculed as a religious fanatic. I wanted to help decent people in other lands to throw off the heavy rule of communism. And I was labelled a McCarthyite because of my opposition to that atheistic government. But the facts are there—persecution of Jews and Christians alike, intolerable conditions for any and all political prisoners. I—"

He interrupts himself, coughing more severely this

time, and then continues, "Do you think God, in His infinite mercy, would introduce me to any of the Pilgrims and Puritans in Heaven?"

"I am sure He would be pleased to do so, Mr. President."

"How grand that would be. I want so much to tell them what I tried to do, to rekindle a little of the spirit of what they intended when they landed on these shores. And how ashamed I am of what the nation they died to create has become. Our air poisoned; our morality shrivelling up, an ugly distortion of their ideal; this land with more places of sin than there are churches.

"You know, good angel, I will enjoy eternity for many reasons, of course, but for one in particular."

"What would that be, Mr. President?"

"That I won't have to talk myself hoarse, that I won't have to fight yet day after day, week after week, month after month, year after year for what is good and decent and Christ-honoring. My spirit isn't weary, you must understand, but my mind, my body, there isn't any strength left."

He dies then, this President of the United States, as I stand by his body, and welcome the spirit that arises from it.

"No pain," he says with wonderment.

I nod.

"How old, how very old my body looks. It is true that the Presidency hastens age more than any other job in the world."

"But no longer," I say. "All that is over now. You will not have to prepare for any further battles with Congress, Mr. President."

"Angel?"

"Yes?"

"I hear some music."

And I do as well.

"Oh my . . ."

Against the background melody of an old Thanksgiving hymn, the President of the United States meets his first Pilgrim . . .

Washington, D. C., reacts with official mourning. Heads of government from all over the world come in under tight security. And yet even so a terrorist incident at Dulles International Airport shows that almost nothing is sacred in the atmosphere of this insane world.

A little girl is standing alone near the front entrance to the airline building where a delegation from England is scheduled to arrive.

Dressed in clothes that make her seem a harmless doll, she is holding a rather large handbag. Every so often she looks up at a passerby and smiles.

At the opposite side of the building, a British Airways plane lands. A total of twenty members of Parliament disembark. The Prime Minister and her husband are also on board, but she has had a slight case of airsickness. The others wait at the gate.

"She is supposed to be made of iron," whispers one of them.

"Please, Harold, do not be sarcastic," an associate responds. "You try to hide how much you really do admire the lady, but despite yourself, you cannot."

The other man is silent.

In a few minutes the couple joins them, and surrounded by security guards they head toward the entrance. The Prime Minister seems quite recovered, walking with a sure step.

As the party approaches, the little girl runs up to the first member of the delegation, and gives him the handbag. She is smiling with the sweetness, the innocence of the very young.

"Please, mister, my mommy—!"

She is unable to finish.

An explosion demolishes a large portion of the building, pieces of it scattering for nearly a mile. Most of those directly inside are killed—as well as many more on the outside, bodies flung in a dozen directions.

Several times the number of those dead are injured, blinded by shards of glass, flesh torn by metal, limbs severed, bones broken.

"A war zone!" says the U.S. government official observing the scene.

And that it appears to be. The terminal is in ruins, girders twisted like a toy erector set abused by a very angry child.

Shattered glass is so deep in some spots that—

Cries fill the air. Sirens form a continuous orchestration.

The Prime Minister has survived, but her husband is dead. She is asked by a member of the Joint Chiefs of Staff who has hurried to the airport if she would rather not attend the President's funeral but instead go directly to her hotel.

"Thank you, sir, but the First Lady needs me at this hour," she replies.

As she walks toward an awaiting limousine, she notices a tiny blood-stained dress, red with white lace at the edges, the body it once covered now in scattered pieces.

"Would that be—?" the Prime Minister starts to ask.

"Yes, madam, it is, I'm afraid," the general replies with ill-concealed reluctance.

"Please, sir, would you take my hand? I feel very weak now."

Reports have spread throughout Washington, D.C., with startling rapidity. Some discussion is given to delaying the President's funeral for a day. But that would create more massive security problems than it would resolve.

The First Lady is there. As are the members of Congress. Even the President's political enemies give him praise. One of them, a senior Senator responsible for defeating some of the President's most cherished programs, begins his speech but cannot continue, his grief beyond suppression.

Hundreds attend from scores of countries. The Russians. The Chinese. The French. The Italians. One nation after another, some for the diplomatic necessity of it, others out of a genuine regard for this man, and out of awareness for the fact that life is tenuous, whether it ends "naturally" or through the act of a terrorist group willing to use a child no one would suspect.

The Prime Minister of England now ascends the podium in front of the White House.

"When I left my native land, I had a husband," she says. "When the plane landed just two hours ago, he and I were planning to spend as much time with the First Lady as we could, given the affairs of state back home. Now, in the midst of this nightmare day, she and I both need to comfort one another.

"Life begins with a miracle bestowed by the hand of God. It ends as we take His hand and He helps us from this mortal body. My husband died in my arms, but he died triumphantly, for his last words were, 'Dear, dear wife, the Savior is waiting, now, for me. An angel attends my way. You must leave me and hurry on, my dearest love.'

"That is in part why I have the strength to come before you now. But it is just a part, however important it is. The other lies in words spoken to me by your President less than a week before his illness claimed him. The words may be familiar to some of you. They are from the Book of Revelation:

" 'And he shewed me a pure river of water of life, clear as crystal, proceeding out of the throne of God and of the Lamb. In the midst of the street of it, and on either side of the river, was there the tree of life, which bare twelve manner of fruits, and yielded her fruit every month: and the leaves of the tree were for the healing of nations . . . And there shall be no night there; and they need no candle, neither light of the sun; for the Lord God giveth them light: and they shall reign forever and ever.'

"*That* is the future, ladies and gentlemen, the only one that matters. Right now, as I speak, the President of the United States and my minister-husband are where no bombs can touch them, no lies can hurt them, no pain can sap their strength."

Tears trickle down the sides of her cheek.

"Forgive me," she says as she collapses into the arms of the First Lady.

The next morning, the Prime Minister of England boards a plane with the body of the man she loved for thirty-five years . . .

Even so, government continues on as always, for the better as well as for the worse . . .

I find prayer breakfasts and an organization called Congresswomen for Christ and other such—wonderful to see, encouraging, of course, but along with them, and in greater abundance are the lobbyists for the various industries whose products have caused a great deal of the pain of the world: the liquor lobbyists; the American Tobacco Institute lobbyists; the ones pushing legalization of marijuana; those who favor making prostitution legal. On and on—a veritable sea of them, foaming with the poisons inflicted by their own "doctrines" in opposition to those of Almighty God.

Does it stun me to find the American Tobacco Institute swarming with demonic activity—no real possession, actually, but slavering hordes of oppressors? I overhear several of them discussing a game plan.

"No one can easily make the case that tobacco in itself is evil."

"That may be true, for the moment, but I would not be excessively confident."

"You are too easily upset. The fact is that we have an ideal environment here that has been working out nicely for years."

"Yes, make smoking socially acceptable. Make it commercially profitable. And help form an organization funded to make it respectable, and keep it that way."

"Marvelous! But that has been only the beginning. The *pain* we can inflict, the suffering!"

This one demon is fairly ecstatic with enthusiasm.

"I thought I had died and gone to Heaven—well, you know what I mean—when I saw that chap coughing his life away from emphysema," he continues. "It was wonderful, I tell you. The blood and phlegm and other stuff gushing out of his mouth. And the suffocation he was feeling because of the damage to his lungs. I was delirious for a long time after that, my thoughts jumping ahead decades to encompass all the possibilities."

Says another: "And the retarded children! Wow! What we fail to abort, we can cripple, we can retard, we can do so much else!"

One demon seems to glow as he adds, "And *then* we zap them with *euthanasia.* I do not know about the rest of you, but I want to be there when they kill the first mongoloid idiot legally!"

They are gleeful, planning a whole monstrous tapestry of mischief to be inflicted during the weeks, months, years ahead.

I visit other organizations, each dedicated to spreading its own "doctrine." My next stop is one dealing with freedom of speech and the press.

I encounter a variety of discussions there, in offices, and behind conference room doors. A man who publishes pornography is discussing his chain of adult bookstores. The lobbyists are nodding in agreement.

"It's a free country, you know," the pornographer is saying. "If I want to show some skin, that's exactly what I'll do. This ain't Russia after all, you know. People get their jollies from the stuff in my stores, you know."

"Exactly," a lobbyist agreed out loud.

"Why, you know, I've doubled the number of private booths. I'm providing a real service, you know. I've even had a special deodorizing system so that the places won't smell, you know, like those gay bathhouses. I've got the best line of plastic toys in the industry. And, you know, the aromatics—just great—a cheap high—and my films and books, you know. What more could the stupid public ask for?"

"Yes, yes, absolutely," a Greek chorus responds.

He opens up an attache case and takes out a pile of magazines.

"These are what America is all about," he says.

"I should say so," one of the lobbyists agrees as he leafs through a copy.

"Just good clean sex," the man says, licking his lips. "I mean, where would, you know, that guy from Lynchburg be, you know, without sex?"

Everyone bursts into laughter.

"Look at those," he says, pointing to a centerfold. "Lust, you know, good old lust. That's what makes this world, you know, go around, guys."

I leave though I would rather have disputed everything he said. I would rather have given him the volumes of police reports that indicated that the majority of all violent crime resulting in death had a sexual base. Not to mention the epidemic of sexually transmitted diseases—the disintegration of families—just the kinds of byproducts that his "good old lust" propagated.

Freedom of speech was never meant to bring about the license to engage in any type of lustful, degrading, demoralizing enterprises, allowed to spread their poison because trying to stop this would be "un-American." I can say that from having visited only a little while ago the men who created the Constitution, spending time by their side and hearing all the reasons behind what they would write, what they would desire for the nation.

And further back, hundreds of years, I was with the Pilgrims and Puritans. I heard the essence of what their vision for America was. A country free of persecution but also a country founded on the premise of a new Israel, a land devoted to God, a land that would be free but a

freedom with different connotations than the word bruit-
ed about in modern times. It was not freedom, they
would have said, looking at the United States of the
current day, for men and women to be enslaved to promiscuous sex, to violence, to drugs. A law-abiding country was not one in which countless numbers broke moral
laws, laws handed down by the Creator. There was *never*
to have been *that* kind of freedom or license. In the days
of the Pilgrims and Puritans, anyone caught in the sin of
adultery or homosexuality would have been dealt with in
exceedingly harsh terms. Too harsh, it might be asked?
Too unloving? Too judgmental? That which is clearly
stated in God's Word, that which is without equivocation
branded intolerable should not be overlooked, should *not*
be permitted by those who claim the name of His Son,
under the guise of not wanting to be judgmental. Oh,
what cancers are allowed to run unchecked in the name
of non-judgmentalism!

I visit other organizations—set up to serve the elderly, the poor, the homeless. Most are strapped for cash;
most have almost to beg for the dollars they need. Yet the
tobacco lobby, the gay lobby, the pro-abortion lobby, others of that ilk seem to have no problem finding dollars,
for their money is carried to them in sacks on the backs
of those dying of lung cancer, and those who are retarded,
and those who head for X-rated films instead of being
with their families. In a world of evil triumphant, a world
of too few good men and women doing too little to stem
the tide, to dam it up so that it cannot spread any further,
in such a world, the Washington, D. C., lobbyists, sustained by those profiting from the moral degradation, are
always going to be ahead, running around like termites

eating into the very structure of society, and helped by armies of workers, with banks of computers and millions of brochures and press releases, and unlimited media access, media controlled by those of like mind and spirit.

And where are the Christians? I ask myself, reflecting on that first, fine family at the outset of my sojourn on Earth. Where is the salt of the earth? Salt is supposed to prevent spoiling. Without the salt, there is decay.

I visit some Christian lobbyists who are having money problems, but some others are not, at least not as severe. They are good at raising money. They are good at spending it. And then the other lobbyists, the unsaved ones who would like to see the hastened disintegration of Christian influence in the United States and elsewhere, take the weapon that has been handed to them, the weapon of financial accountability, and fling it back into the heart of Christianity, and those thus wounded cry and scream and raise a fist at the evil world around them.

I stand, amazed, at one ministry in particular. The head of it lives in a home worth $600,000; he has parties in a houseboat valued at $100,000; his wife has a diamond ring worth $20,000; and he just spent $1,000,000 on designing and building a cafeteria so that, to use his words, "my people can eat in style."

That ministry is located not very far from Washington, D. C. Of course, when you are an angel, distance is of no consequence; but I suppose some of the habits, the conventions about time and such that the human beings around me have, are beginning to affect my own thinking.

In any event, I visit the headquarters of that ministry. I see a fleet of limousines carrying guests about.

"They were donated," someone says in response to another's question, the very question I would have raised if I could have done so. But the money was still spent, I would retort; it could have been used to buy less luxurious transportation, and the difference used to support more missionaries or feed more of the poor or given to other needful ministries—the fact that the limousines were donated is irrelevant under the circumstances. (Was the $20,000 diamond ring donated also? I wonder.)

I see the building designed to house visitors, the hanging crystal chandeliers in the lobby, the plush carpeting, the leather-covered sofas and chairs, the imported marble, the hand-carved statues.

"It was bought and paid for through a special fund donated by our supporters," I hear. Same specious reasoning—millions of dollars siphoned away from the mission field, the stomachs of hungry children, the ministries barely able to pay their heating bills.

And I see one little woman, probably in her late-seventies, wandering around, astonished by what she sees, appalled by it as well. She goes into a jewelry store on the premises, sees a particularly fine-looking diamond ring, and finds out that it had just been traded in by the founder's wife who wanted something a bit more elaborate.

She leaves that store, that building. She walks to a bench in a shaded grove nearby. She bows her head, and prays aloud, "Father, take me from this place."

But the vast majority of those present seem joyous. A group of them is singing a hymn back in the lobby. Others are eating a buffet lunch. A mother is holding her daughter, both of them well-dressed. A brass-plated piano is played by someone in a tuxedo.

Getting up to speak is a member of the hierarchy, a vice president of the ministry, who tells of the need for sacrifice, enabling the Lord's work to continue—while

not letting you know that his salary is $200,000 a year,
and there are others being paid higher sums than that!
How much of an abomination this must be in the eyes of
God is not lost on me. Many people are indeed sacrific-
ing to keep that ministry going. But just that vice president's salary alone requires a donation of $100 annually
from each of 2000 elderly supporters. He lives in a large
$250,000 house, so add another 2500 to that number.
And he has an expense account greater than the income
of thousands of the Christians giving to the ministry. How
pathetic! I scream, realizing that I know those figures
because the man had told them, earlier, to a visitor-friend,
not braggingly, no, not that, but matter-of-factly, which
may have been worse actually. Thousands of men and
women faithfully giving of their earnings or their retire-
ment incomes, thinking that all this is going for the support of missionaries, for example, and not knowing what
is really happening.

Next, there is entertainment. The founder and his
wife appear on a stagelike area in the midst of the lobby.
Other lights darken, and a spotlight is turned on the two
of them. Both are wearing hand-tailored clothes. The
founder's wife has more jewelry than just that one large
diamond ring; her necklace, bracelets, earrings—all are
glittering.

"Everybody enjoying themselves?" she asks.

A roar of affirmation is heard.

Virtually all of those present are caught up in the
atmosphere that is, yes, deliberately constructed, a kind of
retreat from the outside world.

A truth dawns on me. That is the problem. It is a
cocoon of crushed velour and leather and crystal and
diamonds and hand-tailored tweed and brass and so
much else. But the cocoon is not eternal; it is transitory;

from it they must emerge, after a week, even a month, to face that very world from which they have retreated.

"It's a ministry," a guide, beaming, tells one of the visitors.

But to whom? A dying mother from the streets of Alexandria, Egypt—a starving child from the sands of Ethiopia? A missionary from Calcutta, India? And how is it to minister? As an example of what is in store for *every* Christian? Eating in style in a million-dollar cafeteria? Dressing in style? Living in style? Driving in style? Partying in style? The by-products of . . . *faith?*

And what of the times when none of this shields, none of this is there to cling to, to look at, in a sense to hug around the body and the spirit like some gigantic blanket? If this is what faith brings, where is faith when donations drop, when bills cannot be paid, when the diamond ring seems more like a finger raised in a gesture of obscenity?

I leave that ministry sadly. For I sense among those present a kind of substitute for true spirituality. Oh, they are saved, yes, a fact about which I have little question, at least in most of the instances I see, their love of Him obvious. And perhaps this is what really counts, and count it does, but there is more, of course, going beyond the trappings of luxury, that image the world around sees, an image of extravagance, of a Christianity as much based upon the externals of affluence as the internals of salvation, regeneration. Take away the former and there is still the latter, without question, but then it boils down to the quality of life. And how high will be that quality if the externals are eventually gone, replaced by the more mundane, yes indeed, the more typical world known by many more Americans?

I journey on to Atlantic City, a place of glitter in the midst of continuing decay and moral corruption . . .

The man seems old, but he probably is not. His face is so wrinkled that it gives nearly an ancient impression; his hair is straggly, not a great deal of it left. His eyes are bloodshot, his hand trembles as he lifts a soup spoon to his lips. Someone to his right coughs and he mutters something about spreading germs. Finally he finishes the chicken noodle soup and leans back on the folding metal chair, waiting for the rest of the meal. He wipes some specks off slacks that are worn bare at the knees and torn loose from the stitches on the sides. His shoes have served him countless miles of pavement and asphalt pounding, but they will not last much longer. He has 20 cents in his pocket.

The director and his staff do the best they can, but the load is enormous. Each year there is a deficit; each year anxious moments are experienced; each year, the transient population grows, swelling larger and larger, bloated by drug addicts, alcoholics, and those addicted to another pursuit: gambling.

Row after row of cots take up all the space in several rooms. Each one is occupied. A waiting list haunts the director and the other workers.

"We trust the Lord for everything," he says simply to a visitor from out of town, someone interested in helping to support the mission.

The director shows the visitor, a businessman in his mid-forties, around the premises. The work is orderly, effective, but certainly not showy.

"We make the dollars go as far as we can," the director comments. "There is no fat here."

The businessman is impressed. After spending several hours at the mission, he leaves to return home in another state. A short time later, he commits to a regular schedule of donations.

But others, as I find out, are attracted to the glamour of the other ministry and ones like it, caught up in the aura of prospering, and put off by the more basic work of that rescue mission and ones elsewhere across the land.

One man is shaking violently, vomiting over the male staff member trying to help him. The director is called in, decides that they need a doctor for the man. The latter has stopped heaving, at least for the moment. He looks up at the staff member, covered with slop, and at the director and says, his voice hoarse, barely audible, "God does love me even now, doesn't He?" The director replies, "Even as we do."

A doctor comes, gives the man a sedative. In the meantime, the staff member has changed clothes, and the three of them sit in the director's office.

"I don't know how you take all this," the doctor says to the two of them.

"We do it because God wants us to reach out to these men," the staffer replies. "We might *want* to give up sometimes. Throwing in the towel would be easier than cleaning off the stuff somebody has thrown up all over you. But the alternative is to abandon them, and none of us here could live with ourselves if we did that."

The director is obviously, and rightly, pleased at what his staffer has said. He adds only this: "These men have burdens the rest of us will never have to carry. The pain in their eyes is so overpowering with most of them that, well, anyone who is unmoved must be a statue made of stone."

He rubs his chin, an ironic smile on his face as he

says, "Periodically the gambling interests offer to help fund the work. From the beginning we have turned them down. Gambling and allied problems are behind what we are seeing here. We can't accept help from those responsible in the first place."

I leave them, and go outside. It is near dusk in Atlantic City. A line of transients is waiting to get into the mission.

But, I say in words unheard by any of them, where are the diamonds?

I feel utterly alone. I have been alone, of course, from the very beginning, at least in the sense of not being joined by others like me, angels who chose not to follow a new leader. But somehow, now, the loneliness is more pervasive, a mournful dirge all about me, the music that of prostitutes soliciting customers on Atlantic Avenue; of chickenhawks cruising near the Boardwalk; of high-rollers screaming as they lose thousands of dollars; of gangsters in dark corners fixing deals; of the elderly walking the streets because they can no longer afford rents boosted higher and higher by greedy new apartment building owners; of this, and of that, and so much else, a dirge reaching up, I am sure, to Heaven itself.

**P**HILOSOPHER IS DYING.
I hear them talking about that fact. But he himself is smiling, counterpointing their sad expressions.

"I go to be with Him," Philosopher says simply.

Several minutes later, he is "on stage" for his last public appearance, this one in a large college auditorium that has virtually no seats empty, for Philosopher's fame is great. No one in the audience realizes how close to death he is. Only the members of his family and his physicians and his pastor are aware. They had vigorously protested any expenditure of strength on another public meeting, but Philosopher was unyielding.

"There may be one more human being out there

whom the Lord wants me to be His instrument in reaching," he told them. "I cannot disappoint my Savior."

And so he sits, in a softly padded chair, looking at the 3000 students, faculty members, and parents waiting to hear him speak.

"I am honored that you are willing to sit and listen to the ramblings of an old man," he says, his voice normally rather thin, and the loudspeaker system has to be adjusted so he can be heard by everyone.

"I want to present only what God allows me to say. I now await His leading."

He bows his head for a moment, and the audience waits patiently.

Philosopher finally looks up again, tears trickling down his cheeks.

"When I was the age of most of you, I did not know what to believe. How could I look at that which was so apparently real and physical, with form and substance, so that whatever it was could be touched and held, and say that a white-haired old man somewhere in the sky created it all by just waving his hands a few times?

"I could not accept any of that, for it seemed to me the stuff of delusion, and I had managed to convince myself that I was smarter than most people, and, as a consequence, certainly less gullible than the 'religious.'

"I started early with this attitude, I must admit. Usually it hits young people later, in college, as some of you can verify, when they are away from the influence of parents."

And he tells them about the years of agnosticism that plagued him, years of careless living, rather like a prodigal squandering everything in rebellion against his father, except in this instance, he did not even believe that he had such a father.

"And then I stood by my flesh-and-blood father's bedside. He had been praying for me all those years. I held his hand, and remember to this day how very cold it was.

" 'Son,' he said to me. 'I have always been truthful with you, have I not?' I agreed that he had. No matter how much I disagreed with my father, I knew he was incapable of lying. 'Will you believe me if I tell you that there is a God and that, right now, my hand is in His, just as my other is in yours?' My whole sense of rationalism rejected what he was telling me. 'Son,' my father continued, 'why have you kept your Bible if you feel that it is nothing but a collection of myths and legends?' I was stunned. How could he have known that? He might reasonably have assumed that I had thrown it away. 'Son, you marked one passage in particular—Revelation 21:4—why?' I could not answer him at first. Who had told my father? A student at college? A professor? But how could anybody have found out, for one thing? No one had access to that Bible except me, because I kept it locked away.

"My father had been crying until then. Yet even as I looked at him, the tears were disappearing, almost as though Someone were wiping them away. He reached up his left hand, and I took it in mine. 'I love you, son,' he said, his voice getting weaker and weaker. He had been in a lot of pain over the month or so prior to that. And a few hours earlier, he had tossed and turned, little cries escaping his lips. But during those present moments, he seemed stronger. His hand gripped mine firmly, resolutely. His eyes sparkled. 'Dad,' I asked gently, 'how did you know?' He replied, 'I didn't.' Then he closed his eyes and never opened them again."

Philosopher stops briefly, the memories still poignant, his own tears glistening under the glare of over-head spotlights.

"As many of you know, that passage of Scripture is as follows: 'And God shall wipe away all tears from their eyes; and there shall be no more death, neither sorrow, nor crying, neither shall there be any more pain: for the former things are passed away.'

"I wanted to tell myself that it was a kind of delu-sion, that some special mixture of adrenaline and the medicine had revived him temporarily, and the drying of the tears was quite natural. But that still did not explain how my father knew about that Bible and that passage. I had marked it only a few weeks before, long after he had been confined to bed, as a futile hope—at least that is what I considered it to be, an exercise, really—that when my father died, it would not be in a moment of pain, that he would go quietly. We often argued—perhaps debated is a better word—about matters of the spirit, but I loved him deeply, and to have him slip away on a bed of agony would have been intolerable for me. I could not have faced that without going off the deep end, as they say.

"From that afternoon on, I began a slow climb back to faith. A day, a week, more time passed, and I came to believe. Skepticism reared up from time to time, a dragon that had to be fought back constantly. I don't think it is ever really slain. I think it retreats in many of us, waiting for events or circumstances or people or a combination thereof to resurrect it with special ferocity. Becoming a Christian doesn't banish the Devil from us for the rest of our days. It seems to me that the evil one is, rather, driven to a redoubling of his efforts when one over whom he once held sway breaks loose and—"

For Philosopher, there is no doubt that Lucifer is the

root of evil, the instigator of corrosive doubt, doubt that builds up a thick, high wall between the sinner and God.

He stops for a little while, sips some water, closes his eyes again, while praying, and then is ready for another segment of the evening.

"I would be very happy to answer any questions you might like to put to me."

An athletic-looking young man near the front raises his hand, and Philosopher asks him to speak.

"Sir, it has always puzzled me as to how God can be in Heaven, and yet indwelling anyone through the Holy Spirit. How can He manage to be in both of these places at the same time?"

Philosopher smiles and says, "I'm very glad we are starting with the easy ones."

There is a murmur of appreciative chuckling in the audience.

"I believe we can approach the matter in this way. Take a hypnotist—I don't approve of hypnotism and so this example is one with which I am not entirely comfortable, but it may shed a little light on the answer to your question—this hypnotist hypnotizes you, my young friend, and implants within your mind what is commonly called a posthypnotic suggestion. It might be perhaps to eat pickles at midnight or stand in the middle of Madison Avenue and shout, 'The Martians are coming, the Martians are coming.' "

Considerable laughter . . .

"But, whatever it is, that urge is now inside you. The hypnotist snaps his fingers and you are now out of the trance into which he had put you. He stays where he is, which is Fairbanks, Alaska, and you return to your home in Tampa, Florida—many thousands of miles between the two of you. At noon, three days later, you suddenly get up in the middle of chemistry class and announce to everyone, 'I know for a fact now that the world is flat. I almost fell off the edge yesterday.' "

There is no laughter this time because the growing truth of what Philosopher is putting before them begins to become clear to those present.

"There we have it, my friend. That hypnotist is still in Fairbanks, and yet you have just acted upon what his spirit dictated to your spirit. In a very real sense, he resides inside you, and you have just obeyed him."

The teenager continues standing, saying nothing further, pondering the words that have lodged themselves in his mind. He then simply nods twice, and sits down, but he has been reached, indeed he has been reached.

"I will add that in our relationship with Almighty God, the difference is that He actually is within us, whereas only the hypnotist's suggestion has been implanted. And also, I hasten to add, for the hypnotist's subject there is really no choice in the matter—he has been taken over, in a sense. God comes in and stays, true, but He continues to allow us the free exercise of our will. But this illustration, which I heard a number of years ago, is perhaps the closest I personally have ever come to a comprehensible explanation of what the mystery of indwelling is all about."

Philosopher pauses, a jolt of pain hitting his abdomen. He feels abruptly weaker.

But he continues, managing the suggestion of a smile.

"Surely there are other questions?"

Another young man, short, bespectacled, raises his hand and Philosopher asks him to stand.

"You seem to be saying, sir, in more than one of your books, that Satan and his helpers are spreading their influence everywhere. But I thought only God was omnipresent. Would you clear up my confusion?"

Philosopher responds without hesitation:

"Very simple, actually. Have any of your friends been experimenting with drugs?"

"But, sir—"

"You do not have to name them—just tell me if any have done this."

"I suppose they have."

"Where did they get their drugs?"

"Sir, I couldn't answer that here!"

"It is not my intention to have either you or your friends end up in jail or murdered by some member of the underworld, not at all. What I meant was, simply, what sort of person?"

"A pusher . . ."

"Your friends obtain their supply from a drug pusher, is that correct?"

"Yes . . ."

"And then what happens?"

"I don't understand."

"What happens after the drug pusher leaves?"

"They take the drugs, naturally."

"I must correct you, young man. Taking drugs is never natural. In any event, I assume they do this sort of activity either through a vein or their nostrils or through their mouth. Am I right?"

"Yes, sir, you are."

"Do they generally buy enough of a supply to last a while?"

"Yes."

"As much as they can afford?"

"I guess you could say that."

"How many of your friends are addicts?"

"Sir, I don't mean to be disrespectful, but I fail to see what this has to do with Satan."

"You will, you truly will, and that I promise. How many of your friends are addicts?"

"More than I care to admit."

"It is alarming, is it not, when these friends of yours do become addicts?"

"Yes, sir, it is. They're throwing their lives away. I—I try to help them, but it seems almost hopeless."

"And why is that?"

"They can't break the habit."

"It has a grip on them?"

"Oh, yes, absolutely."

"And yet before they met their pusher, it was not like that?"

"Not at all."

"He does not hang around all the time, does he?"

"No, he—"

The young man pauses, a smile of awareness spreading across his features.

"Sir, you mean that once he gives them the habit, they carry it on themselves. If they don't get the drugs from him, they'll find a supply elsewhere."

"That is precisely what I mean, son. And so it is with Satan. He caused our sin nature from the very beginning. He can hook those without Christ—and even many so-called carnal Christians—in the same way a pusher hooks a soon-to-be addict. Once the obsession, the addiction if you will, with sex or drugs or money or things is commenced, all he has to make sure of is that there is a supply around to entice, to maintain the addiction. He does not need his demons for that. He himself is certainly not necessary in this regard. People aid his awful designs—the Mafia with its drug and pornography and prostitution businesses, for example. As you can see, so much of what we have around us is inspired by Satan, but he hardly needs to be on call twenty-four hours a day. Advertisers spend billions of dollars to promote so many sinful desires in order to sell their products that I lost count a long time ago. Satan created this kind of atmosphere, the moral, spiritual atmosphere which we breathe today. A brilliant chap, this Satan, this Devil, this Lucifer; his handiwork saves him a great deal of legwork."

The young man thanks Philosopher and sits down. Next, a girl in the middle of the large semicircular auditorium raises her hand. Philosopher indicates that she can stand.

"Sir, you believe, as you have stated in your books, that most of the media are under demonic influence. Have you had occasion to change your mind about that outlook at all?"

Philosopher does not hesitate in replying:

"I have not. And there are many reasons. But one of the most compelling is what the Bible terms 'knowing them by their fruits.' What are the fruits of the media? Promotion of promiscuity is often the stuff of comedy, winking with approval at that which has generated broken marriages, broken homes, diseases that breed insanity, disablement, and death. And we have the modern spectacle that involves the lifting up of perversion as—"

Shouting occurs toward the back of the auditorium. A young man is standing, angrily shouting at Philosopher.

"Son, I cannot hear very well what you are saying. Would you kindly step up to the front or at least a bit closer, would you do that, please?"

The young man climbs over to the aisle and walks up to the stage.

"I happen to be gay. And I am offended that you referred to my lifestyle as perversion."

"Oh, did I?"

"Yes, you did."

"But all I managed to say was a single word—perversion. You seem to have filled in the rest of that on your own."

Someone snickers, then is quiet.

The boy is momentarily flustered.

"But is it not so? Your books apparently make no secret of how you feel."

"You are correct. But I am far from being the originator of that truth. God is. And His Word is quite outspoken on that subject."

"Sir, I feel that you are wrong."

"But, son, that is the trouble. You do not *know* that I am wrong. Nor do you know, as you undoubtedly believe, that the Bible reflects only the mood of the times in which it was written. You know nothing of the sort as *fact*. You only *feel* that it must be so because you admittedly have feelings toward other men, and these feel quite normal and decent to you. Therefore, you conclude, there is nothing wrong with them. You use feelings as your guide, do you not?"

"Yes, that is correct . . ."

"How many times have you been to a dentist over the years?"

"I don't understand the relevancy, sir, of that question."

"Please, would you be willing to humor an old man and provide an answer to my silly little question?"

The teenager nods, then replies, "Half a dozen probably."

"For cleanings, fillings, that sort of thing."

"Yes, sir. Once I had to have a root canal done."

"Oh, my, yes! I have had more than one of those. Simply awful business!"

The boy adds, in agreement, "I remember one time, it was so bad, the pain, I—I thought I was going to die."

Philosopher stands, with effort, and walks over to the edge of the stage.

"You mean, son, do you not, that the pain was so awful, so intense, that you *felt* as though you were actually going to die? And not as a figure of speech, either?"

"Yes, I—" he starts to say.

"But, lo and behold, you are here now, before God and Man, alive. How accurate were your *feelings* then?"

The teenager can say nothing. He stands for a second or two, looking embarrassed and humbled, and turns to walk back to his seat.

"Feelings are wonderful much of the time," Philosopher says. "Feelings can be God's gift. Anyone who has ever loved—and all of us have—knows what a joy it is to love. But not all kinds of love are proper. Can we love money and still please Him? Can we love another's spouse and still honor Him? Can we love to see naked images in a magazine or a film and have God honor that? Genghis Khan loved power; the real Count Dracula loved to impale little children on stakes. A mass murderer named Gacy loved to lure teenagers to his home and seduce them, and dismember them, and bury them all over his property. More than thirty boys died because he loved to hear them cry in pain.

"Love can be grand, ennobling, persuading men and women toward the finest acts, the most inspiring deeds, the greatest courage, the most honorable intent. But not all that is called love is like that. Can you see this truth? And God has said that those who love wrongly and continue to do so will be punished."

The young man, who has not reached his seat, turns around angrily.

"Sir, surely you are not referring to AIDS?"

Philosopher looks squarely at the questioner.

"Surely, young man, you are not referring to God?"

Philosopher bends down and takes off his shoe, holds it out to the teenager.

"Do you see that?" he asks.

"Yes, it is a shoe."

"It does not fit very well. There is a place at the heel which is rubbing against my flesh. I noticed just this morning that there is a blister."

The young man is silent, a frown on his forehead.

"But I was hasty, wanting to get here on time. While I knew the one shoe presented a problem, I slipped the pair on without really thinking, my haste overriding my memory and, also, my common sense."

"Yes, sir . . ." the boy says a bit impatiently.

"My heel was never meant to have anything rubbing against it in that way. But I have a choice. I can switch to a different pair of shoes, and alleviate the problem, or I can stay with these day after day, week after week, month after month, and at some point I will have worn through to the bone if I haven't caused infection, including gangrene, in the meantime, followed by a spread of that up my leg and eventually throughout my body if I do nothing, even something as desperate, as extreme as amputating my leg. If I keep that pair of shoes, and let the infection spread, and my whole body is riddled with it and, my young friend, I die, is that a judgment from God or the most appalling, wasteful stupidity on my part? Please do not lay at the doorstep of my Lord and Savior what your own blindness forces you to ignore."

It is obvious that Philosopher is very, very weak. He walks slowly back to his chair, and almost collapses into it. His family whispers to him that he must stop.

"I must go in a little while," he says with great tenderness to the audience, looking out over the thousands listening to him. "I am very grateful that you have come here this night. May we make the next question the final one, please?"

Another student, a girl, raises her hand, and Philosopher asks her to come forward.

"Sir, as you indicated earlier, you once could not bring yourself to believe in God. I cannot now, either. Help me, please."

Philosopher speaks, but his voice is barely above a whisper. He motions her to come up to him. She climbs the steps and approaches him.

"I am dying, my young friend. Let me tell you that there is a God, and even as I speak, He is welcoming me into Heaven."

He looks at her, his eyes wide, a smile lighting up his face. He reaches out his hand, and she takes it.

"Your father says to tell you that he loves you, and is happy now."

Then Philosopher's head tilts to the left, the hand drops, and he is dead.

The girl starts to sob as she turns around to face the audience.

"My father," she tells them, "died a week ago. The

last thing he said—he—he said to me was that he prayed I—I—I would—would accept the gift of faith and—and—peace that he wanted to leave behind."

She leaves the stage as Philosopher's doctor rushes to the still, frail form in that chair. But he is no longer there; that suit of clothes has been shed. His spirit has left his body. Instantly he sees me.

"You have been here from the first minutes?" he asks with awe.

"Yes, Philosopher, I have."

"Are you to take me to my Lord?"

I cannot answer.

He turns, looks upward.

"Jesus," he says. "Oh, dearest, dearest Friend."

And he is gone.

OUTSIDE.

The night air is clear. A great many stars are apparent. Memories flood in on me. I ache to return to my home, for Heaven is my home, my birthplace. I have gone through the centuries on Earth, soared the globe, witnessed a whole encyclopedia of people, events.

It is time to—

"Darien!"

I hear the voice as I am walking away from that college auditorium.

I stop immediately, a thin trickle of dread working its way into me, expanding until I nearly continue on, not daring to turn, not wanting to face—

"Darien! Please listen, my friend."

I turn very slowly.

"Hello, Darien. It has been a long time."

DuRong!

I say nothing at first, unable to speak. DuRong, the angel who was closest to Lucifer in Heaven, stands in front of me—and—and—

"You have been looking for my friend, have you not?" he says, smiling.

"Yes, I have, DuRong. Why are you and the others not inside?"

Hundreds of other fallen angels are gathering in back of DuRong. I see them in the darkness, hovering, almost buzzing like a swarm of bees. Most are pathetic in appearance, distorted and twisted and—

"No one was willing to welcome us in," he says, laughing harshly.

He comes toward me.

"Oh, Darien, there is so much to discuss."

"Yes, there is."

"Glad you agree!"

We walk away from the others. He sees me as I cast an apprehensive look at them.

"You have little to fear from them, Darien," he indicates. "You are one of us, are you not?"

A familiar chill grips me.

DuRong looks little different, still quite majestic— the others have changed with shocking totality but not him, so much like Lucifer. His voice is as nearly as rich, as powerful, like all the greatest opera singers and all the finest public speakers ever born, and yet greater even than that.

I begin to feel a hint of old awe, since DuRong is

indeed close to the magnificence of Lucifer himself. While it would be stupid to ignore so much of what I had seen that agreed with all the ghastly stories about Satan, yet other details did not. Why had Lucifer's followers become so loathsome—and DuRong, for one, had remained as grand, as awe-inspiring as ever? Beside him, Michael and the others, including myself, were pallid imitations, reflections in a mirror that had faded disastrously.

"You cannot know how glad I am to see you," DuRong remarks with apparent sincerity. "The others are hardly an inspiration in the remotest sense of the word, but you, Darien, yes, you are very, very different. But, then, I doubt that you realize how very much alike, in every way, the three of us are."

DuRong is casting a spell, I know, but then, like Lucifer he is expert at this, and I am not immune to being drawn to it.

"Let me show you the other side of Earth," he suggests. "I imagine, from the reports Lucifer and I have received, that you have been exposed to the worst that could be seen, the areas where perhaps those serving him may have misunderstood his intentions."

I agree to go with him.

"That *is* wonderful. You make me very happy, Darien, very happy indeed."

The first stop is an opera house. A ballet is in progress.

"That *is* very beautiful," I admit, pointing to the man and woman on stage.

"Both are atheists, you know," DuRong says. "They rejected God a long time ago. That has not stopped them from giving the world discernible perfection in their art.

How magnificently they dance! Why not join me for the rest of the performance, Darien?"

The beauty of their moves across the stage is undeniable. Both are in their prime, slim, coordinated, well-trained. Members of the audience gasp at what they achieve in their art, knowing how very difficult it is, appreciating the self-denial indicated by years of exceptionally hard work.

"It comes only after enormous dedication, my friend," DuRong indicates. "They both get up very early in the morning, and stay at it until late at night. Everything is planned with the utmost care—from their exercising to their ballet practice to their meals, yes, everything. And it has *been* like that since they were quite young."

After the performance, DuRong and I leave.

"There is beauty without God, you know," DuRong says proudly. "In Mankind reservoirs of such creativity, such glorious potential, remain only to be tapped."

After the ballet, we go elsewhere—an opera singer at the Met in New York City; a stage actress giving the performance of her life on Broadway; a gallery in which stunning art is displayed.

"Most of that owes no allegiance to God," DuRong observes. "In fact, a greater number than you can know did their very finest work *after* they shed debilitating guilt, the inhibitions foisted upon them by what *He* demanded in their lives before He would accept them as having any worth at all."

"But, DuRong, that just is not the answer. Is it so wrong to expect them to be moral, to follow the Ten Commandments, to accept His Son into their lives?"

"But the implication *is* that unless they do *all* of

that, they are worthless, like worms plowing through garbage every single moment of their lives."

"No, it is not that at all. They have worth; they have genius, creativity, all that is fine and good. But until they take that final step—"

"There is more to see, Darien," he interrupts.

He shows me a home for retarded children. A treatment center for cancer victims. A hospital specializing in reconstructive surgery for burn victims.

"Very beautiful, is it not?" he says proudly. "Could there be anything more loving, more sensitive, more noble than what you have seen? And, Darien, *none* of it can be attributed to God. All of it comes from Man's own instincts. In fact, the home for retarded children is financed by a lifelong atheist. One of the skin specialists at the burn center had studied at one point to be a priest but came to perceive the inherent inconsistencies in Christianity, Catholic and Protestant."

I keep my silence.

There are other places we visit, DuRong showing them off to me with ill-concealed relish.

We pass by a disheveled man in his late thirties. His clothes are torn, his face and hands very dirty, his hair stringy.

"What about him?" DuRong asks. "Where is God's mercy with that individual? Is that how He treats His blessed children?"

I can stand no more.

Lord, give me the words, take upon Yourself my usual ineptitude, make me a channel for Your wisdom . . .

"He ruined his life, that chap," DuRong has continued. "He is rejected, sick, alone. I fail to see God, socalled loving as He is, doing a damn thing for him."

"It is ironic that *you* are the one using that word, DuRong."

"Which word?"

"Damn."

"Surely you have heard much worse while you have been here? Why does it upset you so?"

"Oh, I have. All of those words probably. The difference is that you and the others are responsible for his damnation in the first place. You put temptation before him; you *created* the gun that *he* has placed to his own head admittedly, but without the gun there in the first place, he would have nothing to use. I speak of a gun only symbolically. It is much broader than that, much more perverse. There is no gun, of course; it is simply another word for the alcohol that has eaten away his inside, that has destroyed his mind. God had nothing to do with that."

DuRong laughs hoarsely.

"Show me what He has done to *stop* what is happening."

"God has offered forgiveness through Christ."

"And that is supposed to solve everything, Darien? I thought you were more realistic than that. If forgiveness means that an Adolf Hitler is going to be in Heaven, I am very glad we left."

"I doubt that Hitler *asked* for forgiveness. But then, now that you mention it, who created Adolf Hitler in the first place?"

"God? Does He not create everyone and all things?"

"True. But what God brought to life was a child He desired to be His own. What made him the Hitler he became was the world you and your fellow demons threw up around him. *You* turned his life upside down. *You* corrupted his mind. *You* twisted a genius into a madman.

And Hitler *was* a genius. Few can deny that fact. That his genius became evil, perverted, diabolical is not the fault of God but of yours, of the others—D'Seaver's, D'Filer's . . . of—"

"You still are not convinced, are you, Darien? You hesitate even in saying Lucifer's name."

"I hesitate because if it is true that he is as malevolent as has been claimed through the centuries, then the Lucifer who once was, the Lucifer whom I once—"

"Loved? Is that what you were about to say, Darien? Why would you have loved someone so deserving of such contempt?"

"Not at the beginning. Then he was—"

"Magnificent? Yes, he was magnificent. He—"

DuRong shivers a bit. I sense the slightest change in his demeanor.

"You just said that if a Hitler could get into Heaven, you are glad you no longer remain there. But what if a DuRong, yes, what if a Lucifer could be washed clean, could be forgiven and return to Heaven as angels reborn, what if God were willing to—"

"And we would have to *submit* to Him? Follow His orders? Do what *He* desires?"

"But God has never changed, DuRong. He has always been willing to forgive. As for submission, what is it now that you are doing? You have submitted to Lucifer's will since the dawn of time. What kind of master has *he* been?"

DuRong is acting with growing strangeness, instability.

"You show me ballet, opera, charities. You point to the beauty of art, the decency that does rest in any motivation to help others. And you indicate that none of those we saw owe any obedience to the Almighty. They have run their lives without Him. And yet you admit that God created each one. DuRong, that which is noble, inspiring, artistic within them was implanted by God in the first place. Talent cannot be taught; it is not a serum injected, a drug ingested, something in the air that is breathed in and takes root. It was instilled even before birth, as a seed destined to grow. Anything good we have seen has come about not because of their atheism but *in spite of it.*"

DuRong says nothing. I notice a surge of moaning among the others. They all have been disturbed.

"Just examine the way you all are reacting now. You know truth. You know it better than a missionary who has spent an entire lifetime of sacrifice in spreading the Great Commission. Take a library of all the books of faith ever written and include even the Bible, and yet your knowledge would transcend five hundred times all that!

"Which is why you work so hard to *corrupt* the very universe itself, why many of you also are out there!"

I make a sweeping gesture at the heavens.

"You would like to destroy all of that, and begin anew, fashion the whole of creation in the image of *your* master. Obedience to the will of another is not the problem. Obedience to the One who gave you life *is*—and so you worship a substitute, preferring the demonic to the divine, someone who promises you what that very knowledge of yours knows to be false. You have read the prophecies and know them word for word. If you were to be honest, you would be confronted with the spectre of your own impending doom, and so you cling to the most awful, the most evil, the most decadent lies ever spawned!"

I sense something else at that point. I hear a distant roar, rapidly getting louder, closer. DuRong and the others are cowering, so frightened that if you could say, with any accuracy, their blood was freezing in their veins, then that would hint at how they are now behaving.

"Enough!"

A single word. Just six letters. Spoken in an instant. But spoken with the most traumatic ferocity of any word in history, divine, demonic or human.

"ENOUGH!"

Again. Stronger.

"*E N O U G H!*"

And in a split second, if time were real, an accurate description, in a split second, there is no ground beneath me, nor sky above, nor fallen angels quavering frenziedly, themselves a blur, nor—

Only . . . around me, vivid, suffocating . . . the reality, the terrifying, monstrous reality. . . of Hell.

At first there is just nothingness. A sound like that of a howling wind sweeps across my consciousness, sweeps through me, causing a chill more profound than any before now. I can still *see* nothing. And I experience an instant of deep, suffocating mournfulness, but even that word does little to describe my state.

I feel what it is like to be in a place without God, cutting aside all the childish rationalism and nihilism of Man, the immature playthings of deluded spirits . . . *experiencing* the inner core of atheism as objective, fundamental *reality* like a vulture swooping overhead, ready to devour.

"Oh, God . . ." I say aloud.

The entire "place" in which I am shudders as though down to its very core.

And then a voice—

"Please, do *not* speak *that* name in *this* place!"

The voice familiar, rich, magnetic, eclipsing even DuRong's, a chill edge to it that penetrates to—

Lucifer.

"Where are you?" I ask, trembling.

"Here, there, everywhere," is the reply.

"I do not understand," I admit.

"You are in my breast. I carry you around as a woman pregnant. I spit you out of my womb at my pleasure."

Laughter.

"You have been hunting me over history. And yet you found me almost from the beginning. You have seen me again and again and not known it. How stupid an angel you are!"

I recall the decadence. The pain. The pungent odor of burning Jews assails me.

"Let me now show you something else . . ."

A scene is played out before me or, rather, a montage of scenes, one right after the other. I am in the midst of a gala party. It is in a ballroom. There are crystal chandeliers, and diamonds, and lavish gowns and—

The alcohol flows freely. So does the cocaine.

I see 2000 pairs of shoes, and dozens of Rolls Royces . . .

"I have them all," the voice says proudly. "Because they do *that* while they permit *this*."

A man, dying from hunger, sits on his haunches pleading with passersby for a morsel of food.

Other scenes, spinning, people at the altar of fame, power, sex.

There had been no real warning about the volcano. No one is prepared. Hundreds die. A little boy runs after a dog whose fur is aflame, screaming for someone to help him until the lava drowns out his thin, agonized voice.

The bodies of many are visible afterwards, some partially covered by the once-red, now-gray molten rock cooling down. Every few feet an arm or a hand is visible among the layer of death, the fingers twisted in pain, frozen that way like Arctic weeds.

A man weaves his way through the hands and arms and other half-buried portions of bodies. He takes off rings, watches, bracelets, puts them in a sack. Some of the bodies are lying on top of the hardening lava. He rummages through their clothes, finding wallets, money belts . . .

"I never caused that natural disaster, but I took advantage of it, Darien. It proved to be an opportunity that I could hardly let pass by, do you not agree?"

The elderly woman is temporarily alone to tend to the family store. Her husband has gone home to get her some more medicine.

Two gunmen blow her head off, and get away with $35.15 . . .

"My workers stayed behind," says the voice. "They wanted to see the husband's expression. It was worth waiting for."

The man is consumed by chills so intense that they seem to infiltrate every inch of his body, every muscle trembling, shaking. His skin is covered with lesions. He weighs barely a hundred pounds.

"Oh, God, why are You doing this to me?" he shouts but never getting an answer—a hundred times a day it seems but only dead, awful silence . . .

"That *is* an achievement, Darien. To get them to blame God . . ."

"Please help me. He's got a knife. Won't some-one—?"

"A dozen witnesses, Darien, And no one helped."

In the midst of the town square, a man is blind-folded. Standing before him are five other men, each holding a rifle. The man is clutching a Bible. It falls from his hands, covered with blood.

"Marvelous, Darien . . ."

Image after image, a kaleidoscope . . .

"My world, Darien. Yes, my handiwork. You are coming to stay with me, are you not? To share . . ."

I am shuddering. So all of it is true, any remaining doubt buried under the weight of the evidence surrounding me. God's reasons—all *true*—Lucifer/Satan's exile—*justified* beyond argument. God knew the end from the beginning, and all else. He could *see*—!

Suddenly there is silence.

I feel extraordinary heat.

. . . screaming.

No more blackness. No more—

I knew, from the Casting Out, and beyond, that Hell existed, knew that it was nowhere near Heaven, knew that the evil ones of history were there. But seeing it, being *in* Hell, watching—

Someone on a table. A horde of fallen angels around him. They have knives. They are cutting into him. The pieces are put into an oven. And then taken out, burnt black, fingers and toes in ashes. And still alive, the body dismembered but moving, a charred tongue protruding from lips blistered and swollen, eyes—

"Oh, please, please, kill me, please kill me now . . ."

The voice is German. The man is Hitler. . . .

And then I am confronted by a creature so loathsome that it could not be called human *or* demonic. It is bent over, almost hunchbacked. The face is rotting, wounds raw, open, with pus dribbling out, gangrenous filth spewing forth like geysers of water from a whale.

The thing is holding a baby's body in its hand, a hand twisted with arthritic ravaging.

It is laughing, this creature, shaking the tiny body like some obscene trophy.

"I have won," it cackles.

I am no longer silent. I cannot be.

"You have not!" I shout. "That is only an old suit, thrown away, useless. That baby's spirit is where it belongs—not here!"

The creature spins around and faces me as it tosses the body to one side.

"Fool!" it says, cackling. "You—"

I realize, with electrifying sudden clarity, who this creature is.

I stumble back as the cackling vanishes, and a familiar rich baritone replaces it.

"Welcome to my world," Lucifer says.

He throws his arms about, indicating the vast reaches of Hell.

"The place of my habitation once was very different, as you know."

Incredibly I detect the slightest trace of regret.

"Give it up, Lucifer," I plead. "God may be willing to forgive you. The Cross that is now the symbol of your defeat could become the instrument of your rebirth."

"You speak with great conviction," Lucifer says wistfully, holding up his hands. "But these have centuries of blood on them. These have destroyed the bodies of Jehovah's saints. These have plunged daggers into the hearts of the unborn."

He points to his head.

"My thoughts have invaded the church, the office, the home. My programs are on prime time, on cable, in syndication. My concepts are on stage. In motion picture theatres. Books. Magazines. There is nowhere anyone can turn without being confronted with *me!*"

Gradually that door of regret is closing, as Lucifer relishes his power, his influence, his . . . dominion.

"Return to subservience?" he begins to shout. "Return to sitting at *His* throne? Worshipping Him? You *are* a fool, Darien!"

He spins around and around.

"You probably see how lovely I am now. You probably think how grand it would be if the golden streets of Heaven were once again graced with my beauteous presence."

As he moves, portions of him erupt like giant boils pierced, sending out gushers of poison, green and yellow and smelling of decay and disease.

"This is but one me," he says. "Let me show you another."

He seems to take off that one self and put on a new one, like exchanging a suit of clothes.

"I am a judge. I undermine the legal system by voting to allow abortions. I permit the release of those who have slaughtered others because some technicality of the law has been violated. And when the public finally votes me out, I hide behind my femininity and play at being a coy little devil, if you will pardon the expression."

And—

"Look at me now, Darien."

The change this time is most startling of all, and at the same time, the most obscene.

"This is the guise with which I am most comfortable, Darien."

He is now a tall, handsome, well-built young man, naked.

"This is more the real me, Darien. Why do you think so many followed me out of Heaven? From envy? From respect? You play well the part of a fool, Darien, but I do not think even you are quite that naive."

He walks toward me, flaunting himself.

"Come to me, Darien. Blend your spirit with mine. Have the kind of experience that—"

I run. I know he is behind me, following me. I take flight through the corridors of Hell. I stumble, fall, flames leaping up at me. The spirits of condemned human beings reach out from cells in the walls surrounding me.

"Release me, please!" they cry.

"He has rats eating me. Please—"

"I am being put on a spit and roasted."

"Spiders—no—no—all over me—piercing me with their—"

I am lost. Everywhere I turn, there is horror. I am in an open room, at the end of one of the corridors. Some poor tormented souls cry out in agony. They are feasting on dismembered bodies, oblivious for the moment. And then they realize what they have been doing, and scream in utter despair and terror until *they* are pulled apart and devoured by others who then comprehend what has happened and hold up their blood-stained hands and—

No, no, no! I scream wordlessly. *I—*

Somehow they have heard, and they turn toward me. They cry in unison, *You are an angel. Please relieve us of this torment. Please take us from this place of damnation.*

I try to tell them that I can do nothing. They advance toward me, picking their teeth with the bones of the dead.

I remain no longer but reenter the corridor. On all

sides there is screaming, a montage of ghastliness, the odors of—

Finally I can go no further. I have reached a dead-end. All around me are flames, rocks glowing red, then turning molten. I trip on a severed head that suddenly looks up at me and laughs insanely—just before it catches fire, the laughter replaced by the screaming of the damned.

I am trapped. It seems I can only wait.

I sense something nearby . . .

Observer!

He is hiding in the shadows.

"For me, there is but an eternity of this," he says in a tremulous whisper. "I have chosen my hell and now I must lie in it. But, Darien, you mustn't do that."

I look about me helplessly.

"Not about, Darien. Not this way or that. Above!"

Ahead I see Lucifer. Gathered around him are a thousand of his demons. As I look, they become one, their forms blending, and at the same time the real Satanic self returns but bigger, even more revolting, red sores erupting onto me, his breath the stuff of cesspools. He raises a hand, commanding Observer, who goes, whimpering, standing before Lucifer, becoming a part of the ungodly union.

And then Lucifer, former comrade of Heaven, now maestro of Hell, turns to me, smirking, his tongue darting in and out of a mouth filled with the tiny bodies of aborted babies being crunched between his teeth.

"Perhaps, Darien, you carry with you the quaint notion that I can be appealed to through an overture to my conscience. Perhaps you think you can reach my heart."

He cackles ferociously.

"Hearts are my fodder, Darien. I enjoy their taste. I wallow in the blood that pumps through them. I add ingredients of my own—some cocaine, a pinch of heroin, a drop of bourbon—that is *my* blood, Darien, and I share it with Mankind!"

He steps a bit closer. I can back away no further.

"Take a look at Observer's book. Examine its pages. He tells all. It is destined to be a best-seller. Millions will read it, *my* millions, when I finally ascend to the throne, and destroy God Almighty!"

He throws the book at me. It lands at my feet.

"You think of conscience. Goodness. Mercy. Silly stuff, Darien. For the weak. My strength is pain, my energy from the bloodshed of wars, my ecstasy from the dying of hope and the birth of despair. Your men of God rant and rave about my punishment sometime someday somewhere. For me, there is no wait. I mete out *my* punishment now. I grow stronger from the cries of starving millions. Plagues are my rejuvenation. I dine on what your redeemed ones call anarchy, barbarism, hedonism. I relish the acts of the homosexual and call them my baptism."

He is very close now.

"Kiss us, Darien," he says. "Kiss us and join us forever . . ."

I have only one act left, the remaining weapon in an arsenal long neglected by skepticism and doubt over the validity of Lucifer's fate. I fall to the molten-red floor of Hell, stirring up the ashes of Eden, and my voice, created by God Himself, cuts through the screams of damnation.

"I claim the name of Jesus Christ, and accept the protection offered through His shed blood."

Instantly Lucifer pulls back.

"You think *that* is enough!" he shrieks. "You think *words* can stop me?"

"Not words alone, Lucifer," I say, gathering strength. "It is what they portend. You *are* doomed. You wallow in the excrement of your foul deeds and call *that* triumph."

He hesitates. His whole being seems to shake to its very core.

"You turn the womb into a graveyard spitting out its dead, and call this a battle won in your war against the Almighty. Your weapons are the bodies of babies with bloated stomachs—your elixir the blood of concentration camp victims mixed with the fluids of perverse acts in dark places of passion. You shout of victory, and yet all you have left is the torment of Hell! Your trophies have become the twisted bones of a demented grotesquerie— your former majesty an eternal mirror held up to the rotting filth that you now call your very being."

My anger is spent. I have only pity left. And I tell my former friend that that is so.

"You are without hope, by your own choice. But as for myself and my destiny, I choose, now, my Creator and yours. Take me back, Lord!"

I feel myself being lifted upward. Through the volcanic-like geysers below, there is for an instant, barely visible, the bent-over shape of a wretched creature falling to his knees and weeping . . .

.

AM NO LONGER IN HELL.

But I have not returned to Heaven, either. I remain in some limbo state, still on Earth, still going from place to place, century to century, like someone caught on a perpetual merry-go-round, unable to bring it to a halt, unable to get off, condemned just to stay there, spinning, spinning, spinning. During one turn, the Dark Ages flash before me, filled with overt demonic activity; during another, I see the Civil War in the United States, whole battlefields of the dead and the dying, blood staining dark blue as well as light grey uniforms, often brother having to slay brother; during yet another spin, I witness the birth of the first thalidomide babies, twisted creatures crying pitifully, pain over their

entire malformed bodies, while profits were being made
on the drug that caused their misery; faster the merry-go-
round goes, dizzying, until I tumble off yet again . . .

I cannot age, but I do feel somehow old as I sit here,
on a mountaintop overlooking the plain where the last
great battle of Mankind has taken place. The bodies
number into the thousands, and blood collects everywhere—giant, deep pools like a titanic wave over the
ground, submerging it. It is possible to drown in blood
down there . . .

I momentarily turn away, the odor so strong that it
ascends the mountain. I try to close my ears because the
cries of the dying are loud enough to form a crescendo
that also reaches me—but there is no escaping the pan-
orama below, either in its sights or its sounds.

I decide to leave the mountain and go down to the
plain where the old prophecies always had been pointing,
with devastating clarity.

Some of the dying have had the flesh literally seared
from their bones, and they have only seconds left, those
that survived at all. They see me, of course—the living do
not—but the dying, suspended, in a sense, between two
kinds of life, indeed see, reach out, beg.

"Please help me, sir," I am asked again and again.
"The pain . . ."

"I know I've been blinded, now, yet I see you anyway. I see—"

Ahead, standing as though on an island uplifted in
the midst of a blood-red sea, are several hundred figures.
I approach them. One by one they ascend. The final
soldier turns to me, smiles, says, "We did the right thing."

I nod.

. . . we did the right thing.

Yes, they did—all of them—that one group of hundreds out of countless thousands.

They refused the Antichrist. And he had them slaughtered as a result, threatening to do just that to any others who might decide to rebel.

And now—

Not one of them bore the scars of how they died— no bayonet wounds, no bullet holes. In their resurrection they had been healed, given the bodies that would be theirs throughout eternity.

But the others share not at all the same end. Every few seconds, more are dying. Bodies piled upon bodies, visible where the blood is not quite deep enough to hide them. I look about, and see hands raised against the sky, like stalks of marsh grass in a bloody inlet. For an instant only. Then cut down.

They also see me. They surround me as I go past, trying not to look at them, their eyes haunted where they yet have eyes. Some do not, seared away, only the empty sockets remain. But they see me just the same. And all turn away, knowing that *they* will spend eternity like that—in agony, flames searing but never fully consuming them.

The scene oppresses. I cannot stand it any longer. I leave, not sure of where to go. I have time at my disposal. I can flash forward a thousand years, two thousand, however many. I can retreat in time countless centuries.

But I have nowhere to go. An irony that presses me down inflicts on me a weariness that is so pervasive it is as though all of history has become a weight threatening to—

It does seem as though an eternity somehow has come and gone since I left Heaven. I have seen more than all the human beings since the first two were created by God. Perhaps only the Trinity has seen more.

Can angels become weary? We never sleep, true, but we have consciousness and the very essence of what we are indeed can be subjected to strain, can indeed wear down, can approximate how humans feel. After all, we are not robots without feeling nor batteries that can never run down.

I feel myself spinning again . . .

"I was blind, but now I see!" says the man walking the twisting, winding street. "And my brother was lame, but now he walks."

Not a significant proclamation perhaps; not as momentous in itself as, say, the Holocaust. Nor at all meaningful against the realization that twenty million babies or more have died at the hands of Whim, Convenience or any of the other demons bedeviling those who decide that killing a baby is not murder.

And yet—

I continue walking. I see a centurion with his son.

"You were dead and yet now we walk together," the man says to the child.

I find others, one, two, a dozen, a hundred, a thousand. Healed during just three brief years.

And then . . . Lazarus.

Christ's good and dear friend . . .

Lazarus alive, walking with his family. Speaking of the warmth of the sun on his skin.

People touched by supreme goodness, snatched from ultimate evil, each a victory, one after the other like them throughout history, in Heaven instead of Hell, walking the golden streets, listening to the sounds of angels . . . *singing.*

I sit down on the side of a hill, next to some sheep in that ancient land. Two shepherds are nearby. I overhear them talking about their simple lives, the quiet, isolated place in which they tend their sheep.

I reflect on my journey, recalling everything from the very beginning. I have seen victory and defeat. I myself was almost seduced at the hands of Lucifer.

I indeed am tired. Normally, of course, there is no such thing as being tired for any of the angelic host. We never sleep. We have ceaseless energy for any and all tasks. But this time it is different for me. Along with it is a sense of shame and regret, that I had not simply believed God but, rather, like Thomas had to see and feel the equivalent of the nail-pierced hands and lanced side and mangled feet.

I look about, seeing the sheep, the sky well-nigh cloudless. I remember something God had told me once, about there being warfare all around, just out of sight. Later, in a world of five billion inhabitants, how many would ever be aware of this contest for their very spirits?

Surely, the vast majority scoff at the notion. Angels? How silly! Demons? Nonsense! A creature named Lucifer or Satan or the Devil? How trite and childish! A skepticism presided over by a special council of fallen angels, their job that of fostering the doubt, the sarcasm, all the careless, tongue-in-cheek media depictions of Satan that only enhanced the phony, carnival-like image with which he deliberately surrounded himself.

Of those who believed, how many would follow after Lucifer, not knowing the truth perhaps but instead attracted to him by the veneer of excitement and thrills and seeming fulfillment, beckoned like moths around a consuming flame, its dazzling colors and brightness drawing them in?

A startling insight grips me as though I had a physical body: most of his deluded human followers, seduced by him, would mortgage eternity and be in bondage without ever knowing that this was so, slavishingly responding to his role as corrupt master puppeteer, pulling the strings and causing them to dance to his commands, mixing in huge globs of guilt and regret and much else so that any message of forgiveness is mitigated, unable to get through, unable to become God's knife to cut those strings of Satanic enslavement. Call it humanism; call it gay liberation; call it chemical dependency; whatever the term, it was but another branch on a tree planted by a Machiavellian gardener.

Breathtaking clarity rushes into my very being at that point. The spirit of the age indeed has taken over Earth, and there are now only pockets of the redeemed, a few areas of spiritual oasis—the rest is a desert of damnation.

The net of delusion tossed about by Lucifer and his followers had caught even me by the hem, so to speak, and I had had a glimpse of what total allegiance could have meant, allegiance to one who deserved only contempt.

Something quite astounding happens to me now. I am near Calvary. A storm is ripping the sky apart. I walk up the side of Golgotha, past the time-carved rock that looks indeed so much like a human skull, past the multitudes gathered at the top. Mary, the mother of Jesus, is there, His brothers, a contingent of Roman soldiers, onlookers including Nicodemus. I stand at the Cross, looking at the pain on His face. I am under the crimson flow now, His blood washing over me, all my doubts, all my rebellion flushed away like yesterday's garbage. I look at myself and I am suddenly very white, very pure.

I wander, later, from that place, my mind filled with arresting images. I was at Calvary. I stood beneath the feet of God Incarnate, His blood providing the missing moment in the scenario of my odyssey.

Suddenly I hear a familiar voice. My head has been bowed. I look up.

Stedfast!

Not a fallen angel. Not a demonic perversion of what once was. My friend from Heaven—here on Earth!

"I have been with you from the beginning," he says. "Call me your guardian angel of sorts."

"But I thought—"

"It is all a bit different from what you did think, my friend Darien. Lucifer was actually sad that you ever left Heaven."

"I do not understand . . ."

"You originally were to have joined him, during the Casting Out. You were as close as that. But you held back just a bit too long. It was then Lucifer decided that you would be more beneficial to him actually in Heaven, and he did not try harder to convince you to be by his side, for eventually he thought you would sow the seeds of a second rebellion, acting as his *agent provocateur* in heavenly places. He underestimated your devotion to God, though. You were torn between God and Lucifer, unlike the others who had no compunctions at all about their choice of Satan over God."

"So when God let me go on my journey, He knew what the outcome would be."

"Of course. But He also knew that you would have to discover certain things for yourself."

"And you followed me in case I really did need help?"

"Two angels are better than one, Darien."

"But I never knew. . . I—I never saw you. Nor did any of the—others. How could that be?"

He looks at me, rather like an impatient teacher at an impudent student, fluttering his wings as a telltale sign.

"Darien, Darien, do not put such limitations on the God of miracles."

We walk for a while, talking.

"Earth has turned into a nightmare place," I say at one point.

"Oh, it has—call it the rape of Eden—but even so you have encountered reminders of what could have been if Lucifer had remained loyal, and not allowed pride to entrap him and the rest of Mankind."

That first family, Millie and Charlotte, so many more, redeemed ones for whom the shackles of the sin nature were eventually replaced by the true freedom of being born again.

"You know," Stedfast says, as though reading my thoughts, "so many men and women talk of freedom. They want to have no restraints whatsoever. They want to be free to have sex whenever, wherever, and with whomever they please. And then the sexually transmitted diseases started to put a real dent in *that* thinking, of course: herpes, AIDS, syphilis, and so on. That kind of alleged pleasure brought punishment inexorably along with it. They blamed God, but it was simply the nature of their bodies, the biological realities of being human. Each of them dug their own special grave just as surely as though they had taken a gun to their head and pulled the trigger.

"That is not freedom. That is but a death sentence—they spend the last few months or years of their lives waiting for the execution. The flamboyant piano-playing entertainer, the black ballad singer, the leading-man actor, the rotund veteran TV star, so many other celebrities—the media reports everything. And the message is loud and clear. But, Darien, it is not being heeded, not really. Unfortunately, all of them are under total delusion.

"So there is *no* freedom in *their* freedom, not a freedom that has any validity, for even while it is being shouted from the media as the lifestyle of choice for millions, all of them are in a prison—the bars may not be metal, although sometimes that is the case—and they will go on with that cry of freedom mocking them to the grave and even beyond!"

We wander to Joseph's tomb, go inside, stand by the hard rock shelf on which rests Christ's body. He is passing from death to life even as we watch. Finally He sits up, then stands, smiles at me, and says just five words, "Now you know the truth . . ."

"Yes, Lord, I know the truth," I manage to reply, barely able to say even that, aware of the moment to which I am witness.

A short while later, someone approaches from outside.

A woman.

Our eyes meet.

I find myself saying, "He is not here, the one you seek. He has risen, as He promised."

It is as though the light of Heaven is on Mary's face, her expression sublime.

I watch her go. My whole being weeps with the joy of redemption profound, redemption purchased in blood for all of humanity and which included mercy for a foolishly errant angel.

A voice, rich, kind, familiar . . .

"Darien, are you truly ready now?"

"Yes, Lord, truly . . ."

I AM BACK IN HEAVEN, *as suddenly as I had left. But whereas I left without fanfare, as though sneaking out, hoping no one except God Himself would see me, I return as the hosts of Heaven stand before me, trumpets sounding.*

My fellow angels are spread out in front of me, the assemblage going on further than I really can see. The fluttering of their wings seems so loud that only the trumpets can compete.

Heaven is never dark, no clouds blocking the sun. But in that moment I perceive more brightness than I can remember, an illumination so clear and clean that everything is asparkle.

Moses comes to me, smiling.

Abraham stands before me.

Jeremiah. Peter. John. Constantine. Florence Night-
ingale. D. L. Moody, Countless thousands of believers
over the centuries welcoming me back.

And then the Holy Trinity.

What Man finds so difficult to comprehend is before
me in reality, the only reality that counts.

I fall to my knees in humility and shame.

"Arise, Darien," God says. "This is a time of rejoic-
ing. All of Heaven, angel and human, welcomes you for
eternity. Shame is of earth. It has no place here. There is
no need any longer."

. . . no need any longer.

How those words wash over me, cleansing me . . .

I am standing next to a woman who seems always
to be smiling.

"It's so wonderful," she says, "so wonderful to see
that they have no more pain or want or fear."

She asks if I would sit down with her, and I gladly
answer in the affirmative.

"There were indeed times when I wanted to give up,
the strain was so awful," she admits.

"In what activities were you engaged?" I ask.

"I took upon myself missions of mercy. There were
so many of the poor who were dying in the streets. I went
to them and bathed them and gave them food. So many
children! Their poor little arms were bone-thin. Their
eyes were as mirrors of the suffering they underwent. I
remember, out of the multitude, one child in particular.
His name was Johann. His parents gave him that name
because they had a single luxury—a little battery-operat-

ed record player and an old scratchy recording of one of Johann Sebastian Bach's compositions. When they could no longer give their son even a crust of bread, they left him by a highly traveled road, hoping some stranger would take pity on him. When I saw Johann, the battery had run down, but the player was still there, the record on it, covered by dirt.

"I held him in my arms and took him to our mission. There was no doubt in my mind that he was dying. The ravages of malnutrition had claimed him too severely for too long. He couldn't even hold food in his stomach. Once he vomited it up over me and my helper. And he was very embarrassed, but I told him not to worry.

"We found a battery for the player and kept the record going again and again. As soon as he heard it, his crying seemed to subside into a low, sad whimper. Finally he closed his eyes, but just before that, he looked at me, seemed to become very much stronger and put his frail arms around me. He whispered just one word in my ear."

"What word was that?"

"Heaven . . ."

She pauses, then: "I noticed something I hadn't before. His right hand had been knotted up, gnarled actually. As the life flowed from him, that hand relaxed and opened, and I saw, lying against the palm, a tiny, tiny cross. The pain was gone from his face, leaving only the most beautiful smile I have ever seen.

"And, you know, I left my earthly home a few years later. I closed my eyes to the poverty around me and opened them to majesty. Johann was waiting for me beside a wonderful lake with a sheen like polished crystal. He was tall, handsome, strong. And he introduced me to his mother and his father.

"If only those who doubt could see what it is that we have here, if only—"

She looks ahead, smiles.

"Johann's calling. Will you excuse me, please, Angel Darien?"

"Yes, of course. Oh, what is your name, dear lady?"

"Theresa," she says.

I see her join a tall, handsome young man not far away. He is not alone. A thousand others have joined him, gathering around this woman named Theresa . . .

I meet others, as I would be doing for the rest of forever. I share their joy, it becomes my own, and we rejoice together.

There is a man named William.

"It was indescribable," he remarks with radiance. "It swept over me like a sudden tidal wave, yet it was quite gentle; rather than knock me down, it lifted me up. My mind soared then, not just my spirit. All the shackles of mortality fell away. It is difficult for me, now, even to remember what hatred was like, to realize that once I was subject to the most unreasonable jealousy and outbursts of temper, that I polluted my body as well as my mind. All lust is gone. All impatience. All anger. Everything else that was a stench in the nostrils of a holy and righteous God.

"All gone. Drained from me like poisons from an unhealing wound. These sins have vanished. To be cleansed before Him, to be as white as snow, to know that I am *acceptable* to my Creator—how magnificent that knowledge, that assurance, that fulfillment of what He has been telling the Human Race for so very, very long.

"And I know, if ever the awareness of such things should reenter, it would be merely in the light of my scorn over them, my astonishment that I had permitted God's creation, my body, to be tarnished with the garbage of man's corruption."

He repeats an ancient prayer that he had read a long time before:

The gates of the sanctuary may Michael open,
And bring the soul as an offering before God;

And may the redeeming angel accompany thee
Past the gates of Heaven, where Israel dwell;

May it be vouchsafed to thee
To stand in this beautiful place;

And thou,
Go thou to the end

For thou shalt rest,
And rise up again.

"I carried that with me, in mind and heart, for many years, thinking about the promise it offered. But, now, the reality is ever so much more . . .

"To stand before my Lord, my Savior, to experience fellowship with Him after all the prophecies in the Bible—and hundreds of sermons, and the anticipation of a mortal lifetime—to have Him call me by name! Do you know what I'm trying to say?"

I answer, with utter tenderness, that, yes, surely I do know what he means.

He stops, then adds, before going elsewhere, "God bless you, Darien."

"He has, my friend . . . infinitely."

God requests that I meet with Him. I am there in an instant.

"There is something I must ask you to see," He tells me. "I know it will not be easy, Darien. Are you willing to join me?"

"Yes, Lord, of course I am."

We stand before what I could call a door except that it is not of wood and metal hinges. It is without actual substance but a door nonetheless.

"I want to show you the future, except for us it is now the present," God says not harshly.

"Yes . . ."

I witness a broad overview of the Battle of Armageddon. I see, again, the lone regiment refusing to continue. They put down their rifles. Ordered to pick up the weapons, they steadfastly refuse. As a result they are shot immediately.

"Even in the midst of such an event, there is redemption," I say aloud. "My own journey now seems more needless, more blind than ever. I gave up nothing but my doubts. Look at *their* sacrifice."

"But that was the whole point, Darien. Those very doubts were the seed of your rebellion. In Lucifer's case, his pride compounded the problem—and the two brought about his doom. Those men gave up allegiance to the Antichrist. You gave up what could have become your eternal commitment to Satan. You fought against what could have been, and won, Darien. I am very proud of you."

And the Devil that deceived them was cast into the lake of fire and brimstone, where the beast and the false prophet are, and shall be tormented day and night forever and ever.

A trumpet sounds. The heavenly hosts sing with great glory. I am allowed to see the final moment of judgment on all the fallen angels—Mifult, D'Seaver, D'Filer, Observer, each and every one on the rim of the lake of fire, and then over the edge. Finally Lucifer himself. He turns, and sees me. The defiance is gone. But not the results of countless centuries of deviltry. His countenance is even worse—however, instead of the flaunting of his powers, the perverse pride in what he has caused, there is only terror as he hears the cries of his fellow angels like a thick fog swirling around him.

"Darien . . ." he starts to say, strangely pitiful. "Even now, God knows even now, I cannot come to Him on my knees and ask Him to forgive me. The same guilt I inflicted on others is like a thick wall between us. I—"

He turns, dancing flames reflected on that cankered face, and then he is gone.

And I saw a great white throne, and Him that sat on it . . . and I saw the dead, small and great, stand before God; and the books were opened: and another book was opened, which is the book of life; and the dead were judged out of that which was written in the books, according to their works. And the sea gave up the dead which were in it; and death and hell were cast into the lake of fire. This is the second death. And whosoever was not found written in the book of life was cast into the lake of fire.

Countless multitudes follow Lucifer—those who

obeyed him in life were to share his miseries in the final death. For them all, Hell proved to be just a way station before their ultimate destination . . .

How much "later" is it?

Can such thoughts be answered in eternity?

It is unknowably later, perhaps that will suffice. I stand before God at His beckoning.

"Your walk on Earth was akin to that which many human beings take, from doubt to pain to redemption. It has been so ever since Calvary, Darien. But never before has *an angel* journeyed as you have and come back. Wherever you have been, Darien, the path has been marked. And it will be called Angelwalk, throughout the totality of eternity."

God motions me forward a bit.

"Earth is different now," He says, peering down from His throne, seraphim fluttering.

I sense what is happening. That moment toward which all of history had been heading!

"It is time, is it not, Lord?" I say with thrilling comprehension.

"Yes, Darien. Join us and we go together."

I stand with Father, Son, and Holy Ghost. We pass through the Gate, into the bright, golden sunlight of the new Eden.

EPILOGUE

IN THE TINKLING LAUGHTER *of a particular moment amid the journey of that special hour if time were any longer time, there is found beside that path of legend called Angelwalk what surely must have been a treasured book of the ancient past, pages nearly gone, lying near a kindly lion's paws at temporary rest. Only some meaningless old scraps remain, none displaying anything legible except the last fragile bits of a few lost words.*

A Bo.k of the Da.s of Obs . . ver, Once an Ang—.

Then it is gone in dust, trod underfoot by lions and lambs and bright-faced redeemed led by joyous cherubim travelling Angelwalk toward a golden temple rising out of the mists atop a majestic mount called Sinai. . . .

Finis

AFTERWORD

Now that you have read *Angelwalk,* how do you feel?

Maybe you feel as I did after I'd finished reading the proofs: like I'd been bruised by something beautifully brutal.

The book is beautiful, no question about that. But chapter after chapter, I found my admiration turning into indignation. One minute I was smiling at a deft phrase, and the next minute I was weeping. I couldn't help it.

I told Roger that *Angelwalk* was like a lovely spider's web—made out of steel cables, charged with high voltage.

If this book has moved us, then there's no escape. We're trapped.

There's only one thing left. It's to ask, "Lord, what will You have me to do?"

And mean it.

Warren W. Wiersbe